FI

"Well, well, well." Ro———————————Dad said he had a surprise, but I didn't expect this." Holly lazily followed her brother's glance.

Michael Williams stood just beyond the doors. He glanced up as if he could feel someone watching him and looked directly at her.

For a moment, Holly felt as if he could see through to her very being. Suddenly, the room seemed warmer and the air a little heavier. A sense of anticipation spread through her body. Holly had been around handsome men before, but she had never before experienced the overwhelming attraction that she felt for this man. She took a sip of wine and told herself to ignore him, but she found herself drawn to his gaze; she couldn't stop looking at him. Her hands tightened around the glass as he moved in her direction. She watched spellbound as he walked with an easy, sexy stride that made heads turn as he made his way through the room.

Holly vaguely heard her name being called, but she couldn't take her gaze from Michael. He was tall, handsome, and— she decided— very, very dangerous.

"Hello, Holly." He stood before her.

"What are you doing here?" she asked breathlessly, trying desperately to get ahold of herself. "I saw the guest list and you weren't on it."

He tilted his head toward her and gave her a lazy smile. "I came here to see you."

* * *

Fire and Ice
Carla Fredd

PINNACLE BOOKS
KENSINGTON PUBLISHING CORP.

PINNACLE BOOKS are published by

Kensington Publishing Corp.
850 Third Avenue
New York, NY 10022

Pinnacle and the P logo Reg. U.S. Pat. & TM Off.

First Printing: October, 1995

Printed in the United States of America

This book is dedicated to:

My mother and father, Cecil and Earnestine Fredd, who always told me, "Little girl, you can do anything that you want to do";

My cousins, Christy E. Christain and P. Michelle Christain, for being their own crazy selves;

Daphne Y. Jones, Robyn Ballenger, Sharon D. Jones, Sheryl Armstrong, and Vera G. Glenn, for being great friends and giving me a swift kick in the rear when I really needed it; and my critique group, Angela Benson, Ami Vonesh, and Bridget Anderson, for their unfailing support.

One

"Ms. Aimes! Ms. Aimes!" A group of reporters and photographers ran across Holly Aimes's yard to corner her at the front door. Their breath formed puffs of smoke in the cold, February morning air.

"How do you feel about the marriage of Trey Christian and Marla Johnson?"

"Did you know he was seeing other women while you were engaged?"

The questions were fired at her like bullets from an automatic weapon. Holly's heart raced. She knew from experience how coldhearted and single-minded reporters could be when a melodramatic story like hers came along. The interview she and Trey had given a few days ago about their engagement had appeared yesterday in a local Atlanta newspaper. This morning, she'd learned that her fiancé, up-and-coming actor Trey Christian, had married supermodel Marla Johnson last night in Las Vegas.

Holly took a deep, calming breath before she pulled up the collar of her black wool coat. She walked quickly from her small brick home toward the detached garage, dodging outstretched microphones and bumping into reporters.

One reporter asked, "Have you heard from Trey Christian?" She recognized the raspy voice. It belonged to the same reporter with whom she and Trey had spoken a few days earlier at Trey's house. The question was like salt in the wound of her broken heart. She blinked back the tears that threatened to fall. Her calm expression, like a fragile mask, hid the hurt and pain of Trey's betrayal. Only pride kept her walking silently to her car.

The garage seemed a million miles away, and the group of reporters formed a tighter circle around her. She tried to block out the rapid-fire questions and concentrate on reaching her car, but she could feel a cold wave of panic rise up within her.

"No comment." Her voice was barely audible over the noisy crowd. She kept her head down, focusing on placing one foot in front of the other until she finally reached her car. Her fingers trembled within her black leather gloves when she tried to insert her key into the door of her two-year-old Honda Accord.

"Miss Aimes, could you tell us . . . ?" The noise of her car's engine blocked out the rest of the question. Holly put her car in gear and backed out of the driveway.

As she drove away, tears rolled down her cheeks. She remembered the plans she and Trey had made since their engagement a week ago. The happiness she'd felt during last week's interview seemed like a dream to her now. Today, this cold Monday morning, Holly had to face the fact that Trey Christian had never loved her.

Holly entered the highway and headed north to

her parents' home. She knew that another group of reporters might be there, but her father, Sen. Robert Aimes, knew how to handle the press. Holly brushed the tears from her cheeks. She had been careful, so careful, to stay away from the media . . . until last week. Her family had always enjoyed the spotlight, but she wanted no part of it. Now, she would have to endure the constant questions, the photographs, and the total lack of privacy— all while her heart was breaking.

A strong gust of wind shook her car. Her hands tightened around the steering wheel in an effort to keep her car under control. She had to get to her parents' house. They would know what to do.

Six months later . . .

Why was she still here?

Holly Aimes dropped the ballpoint pen on top of the neatly stacked papers on her desk. She closed her eyes and leaned back in the leather executive chair. Her mind hadn't been on work all morning. She'd raced from Conyers, her father's hometown, where she and the rest of her family had been featured in his latest political campaign ad.

When she'd finally arrived in the Atlanta suburb of Decatur, she had dashed from her cool, air-conditioned car into the three-story, smoked-glass office building that housed Security Force. She and her partner, Pamela Moore, had started the company four years ago, when Pam had abruptly left her family's security business in Alabama and Holly had been passed over for a promotion for the third time at the engineering firm for which she'd worked since graduating from college.

This morning, she had gone directly to Pam's office, eager to learn the outcome of the meeting Pam had attended.

"Well," Holly said, walking through the doorway of her partner's office. "What did they say?"

Pam pointed to one of the chairs opposite her desk and continued with her telephone conversation.

Holly dropped her briefcase onto one of the two Queen Anne chairs. She took off her navy linen jacket and laid it on top of the briefcase before sitting in the other chair. Holly sat with her shoulders back and chin up. Years of Mrs. Howard's School of Etiquette had taught her to appear cool and controlled under any circumstances. The only sign of impatience was the steady tap of her navy low-heeled leather pumps.

As she waited for Pam to finish the call, she desperately hoped that Pam had good news. A lot was riding on the bid they had submitted to the Milton Group.

Originally, Holly was to attend a meeting with Milton Group employees, but at the last minute, the filming of her father's political campaign ad was moved to the same time. No amount of pleading with her father, his campaign manager, or her stepmother would get the date changed. In the end, Pam had gone to the meeting alone.

Holly listened to Pam's end of the conversation. Pam was in her element, selling. Her straightforward, never-give-up attitude was the reason they'd become friends while taking a calculus class at Georgia Tech. It was also the reason they had so many clients.

She and Pam were totally different. One of their clients referred to them as the odd couple. Holly had inherited her mother's dark brown skin and coffee-brown eyes. She wore her thick black hair in a simple shoulder-length bob with a part on the right. She was the technical guru of the company. Designing complicated security systems at a reasonable price was her forte. Holly loved the solitary work associated with engineering and testing computer-based models of her security systems. If she didn't have to talk to her clients, that was fine with her.

Pam, on the other hand, loved working with clients. People were surprised to learn that she had an engineering degree as well as an M.B.A. Many of their male clients were distracted by Pam's beauty when they saw her for the first time. Her eyes were tilted up slightly at the corners like the eyes of a cat. Their color was almost the same light golden brown as her skin. She wore her brownish-black curly hair swept up from her perfectly oval face, with fat ringlets of curls lying carelessly down her back.

Holly would never have worn the bright yellow-green silk dress Pam was wearing today. The navy linen pantsuit was more her style.

"We're still in," Pam said, when she finished the call. Pam opened a drawer in her cherrywood desk and gave a manila folder to Holly. "There are only ten companies left. The next cut is in two weeks."

Pam rose and sat on the edge of the desk. "During the meeting, the bid coordinator and the director of security said that our package looked good. The director said he'd be very surprised if we didn't make it to the next cut."

Holly opened the folder, scanned the top page, and smiled.

"Pam, we're going to win this bid. We've beat out eight of the ten companies in previous jobs, and the remaining two don't have the customer-satisfaction rating we have." She looked up from the paper. For the first time since they'd submitted their bid, Holly felt confident that their company would win.

"I'll admit that it looks like we have a good chance of winning this bid, Holly, but we haven't won it yet." Pam stood up from behind her desk and walked to the window. "We've got to make sure we don't make any mistakes between now and when the bid is awarded."

"Wait a minute." Holly studied her partner. "I'm the pessimist in the company. Why are *you* so down?"

"I found out that three companies were thrown out because they had too many customer complaints. The people at the Milton Group are checking every complaint filed by a customer." Pam frowned and stared out the window. "With us installing security systems in two high-priced subdivisions, I think we stand a good chance of having at least one person who's dissatisfied. I know how much winning this bid means to you, Holly, but I don't want you to be hurt if we don't get it."

Holly laid the folder on the desk. "We've got to win this bid, Pam." Holly thought of the reporters who were parked in front of her house again this morning. She remembered the whirring of camera motors and the flash of lights as she drove from her house. "I can't take the constant hounding by the press."

"But this is an election year. With your father ahead in the polls, the press should ease up on you."

"You know better than that." Holly straightened a nonexistent wisp of hair. "As long as Trey and my father are newsworthy, the press will know who I am and they won't give me any peace." Holly folded her arms across her chest.

"Thank goodness the election will be over soon," Pam said.

Holly shook her head. "No! This is it. I can't take it anymore. I'm moving far away from this zoo and starting a new life in Seattle. As long as I'm in Georgia, I'll be a public figure with no privacy at all."

"But do you have to move so far away?" Pam asked with concern. "You don't know that the press won't bother you if you leave, and Seattle is so far away."

"I need to put as much distance as I can between Trey and me. It's too easy to get a story with us in the same city. I've tried to stick it out. Now, I just want some peace."

"Holly, I've never known you to run from anything. Why run now? The press will stop bothering you sooner or later."

"Pam, when was the last time you had your private life on public display? Have you ever had reporters follow you from your front door to your garage, holding microphones in front of you?" Her tone was filled with frustration. "That happens to me all the time."

"But—"

"I don't want to hear it," she said, standing up. "This time next year, I'll be an anonymous citizen of Seattle. I won't have to walk out my door and see reporters, and my picture won't be splashed across the newspapers. I won't be a public figure anymore." Holly went to the chair and picked up her jacket and briefcase. "But we've got to win this bid first."

"There's not much we can do but wait. We've submitted our best price and warranty. The only open-ended part of the bid is our customer satisfaction report."

"We'll just have to keep all our customers satisfied," Holly said, heading to the door.

"Ha." Pam walked back to her desk. "When you figure out how to do that, let me know."

I *will* keep the customers happy, Holly thought, putting aside the memory of this morning's conversation. She glanced at the clock on the wall. It was six P.M. She looked at the stacks of reports on her desk. There was no way she could give them the attention they needed now. She gathered the reports and put them in the desk drawer. Tonight, she decided, she was going to take a rest from work. No working on proposals at home for her. Instead, she was going to throw a bag of popcorn in the microwave and finally watch the video she'd rented once before and had had to return without watching.

She grabbed her briefcase and left. When she walked past the room where technicians manned the customer support telephone lines, she paused briefly to say goodnight.

"Holly! Wait." Wanda Johnson, the head technician, waved her over to her cubicle. "There's a really irate customer on line two. I tried to get him to tell me the problem, but he said he's called before and he's still having trouble with his system. He said he wants to speak to either the owner or the president."

"That's okay, Wanda. I'll talk to him."

"Do you want me to stay on the line?" Wanda asked.

"Yes. I don't want to irritate him even more by making him repeat what he's told you." Holly went to the empty cubicle next to Wanda's and picked up the line. "This is Holly Aimes, co-owner of Security Force. How can I help you?"

"Ms. Aimes, I'm Michael Williams . . ." Wanda spun around in her chair and mouthed "Michael Williams." "Your company installed a security system in my house that has given me nothing but trouble."

"I'm sorry you've had problems with the system." Holly sat and put her briefcase down. This wasn't going to be a quick call. "Tell me what's happened."

"Your company's been out here twice. If your people can't find what's wrong with the thing, then how am *I* supposed to know? I've set it off three times already. Do you know what the fine is for setting off the alarms in Fulton County?"

"Mr. Williams, Security Force will reimburse you for the fine, and I'm sure we can solve the problem without causing you any more aggravation. Why don't I send someone out tomorrow morning—"

"No, I don't want you to come out tomorrow. You get somebody out here now!"

"Mr. Williams—"

"Ms. Aimes, I want this taken care of now. If you can't do that, then I want this system out of my house."

Holly pinched the bridge of her nose and felt the muscles tighten in her neck as stress began to build within her. With this client, their one-hundred-percent customer-satisfaction rating would go right out the window, and so would their chance of winning the Milton Group bid. "I'll send a crew to your house now." She prayed that not all the vans were out on other jobs.

"They'd better fix this thing—"

"Your system *will* be fixed, Mr. Williams." Even if I have to fix it myself, she thought. "Our crew will arrive within the hour. I'm sorry for any inconvenience this has caused you." She put down the phone, removed a notepad from her briefcase, and began writing. "Wanda, I want you and John to go to Mr. Williams's house."

"You want me," Wanda said, pointing her finger at her chest, "to go to Michael Williams's house?" At Holly's nod yes, Wanda shouted, "Thank you, thank you, thank you."

"You can thank me later. Just make sure that his system is repaired *tonight*. I don't care how long it takes."

"Do you know who that was?" she asked in awe. "That was Michael Williams. *The* Michael Williams."

"It doesn't matter who he is." Holly searched the room for the other technician. "Where's John?" she asked, when she didn't find him in the room.

"This is final exam week at Georgia Tech. He won't be in until next week." Wanda gathered her equipment from the cubicle and looked at Holly. "We're short on experienced technicians tonight."

Holly looked around the room. Wanda was right. That meant she would have to go. "So much for a quiet evening at home," Holly mumbled.

Holly felt as if she was in a sauna when she went outside to help Wanda load the company van. The navy linen pantsuit she'd worn earlier had been replaced by the standard uniform of Security Force technicians— a short-sleeved khaki shirt with the company logo on the pocket and khaki twill pants. With the high humidity and hot July temperatures, the uniform was more comfortable and practical for the varied situations at customer sites. She'd worked in dark, musty basements of one-hundred-year-old homes as well as the pristine attics of brand-new houses.

At seven that evening, the sun hung low in the calm summer sky. Wanda drove as they traveled the lonely highway heading south out of Atlanta. Once they had passed the airport, the scenery changed from row after row of industrial office parks to farms and large wooded areas. By the time they arrived at the guard station of the Atlanta Club, Holly felt as if she'd heard every news item written about the life of Michael Williams. Wanda told her how he had moved from Los Angeles four months ago because he had been offered an outrageous salary to produce his late-night talk show here in Atlanta. She'd heard about the family he'd left behind. When Wanda started talking about the different women in his life, Holly felt that she'd heard enough. "Wanda! No more, please! He's just a man. You sound like you're in love with him."

"Holly, we're talking about the man voted the sexiest black man in America for . . ."

"Two years in a row," Holly singsonged along with her. "I know, you've said it at least three times since we left the office."

Wanda lifted her eyebrows. "Tell me you're not a little excited about seeing him."

"He's a customer— that's *all.*"

Wanda shook her head and turned on the blinker. Holly looked out the window. After leaving the guard station, they drove past mile after mile of wrought-iron fences. The Atlanta Club wasn't like any other subdivision in Atlanta. It had been developed with the rich in mind. The smallest home sat on ten acres of fenced-in land. Houses were hidden from the street by perfectly manicured trees and shrubs. No expense had been spared in developing this community. It was home to many of the city's elite, high-visibility families.

The lifestyle was one that Holly now avoided. During her involvement with Trey, she'd attended dozens of parties, dinners, and coming-out balls. What she'd witnessed at those events, the back-stabbing and the constant drive for success, had made her want to stay away.

Security Force was one of only five companies asked to submit a bid to install security systems in the area. Holly smiled as she remembered the celebration she and Pam had had when they'd won. That win had led to a steady stream of work for their company . . . and work meant money. Money was exactly what she needed to open another branch of Security Force in Seattle. Winning the Milton bid would bring in enough money to do that. But first, they had to take care of Michael Williams.

The van came to a stop at his gate. Wanda rolled down the window and pressed the button on the call box. Holly watched in satisfaction as the lens of the surveillance camera moved back and forth. Three cameras in three different locations were focused on the gate entrance. At least the cameras work, she thought, as she listened to Wanda give the company name and hold out her identification so the camera could capture it on videotape.

A few seconds later, the gates opened and they drove through. Any other time, Holly would have been impressed by the professional landscaping and the feeling of isolation created by the abundance of dogwoods and magnolias. Today, she looked for surveillance cameras, motion detectors, and lights. Everything seems to be okay, she thought, as they rounded another curve of the driveway.

"Uh-oh," Wanda gasped.

Holly turned her attention away from the passenger window when she heard Wanda. "Lie to me and tell me that's not a police car." Holly closed her eyes and leaned her head against the headrest of the minivan. The stress-induced pain across the bridge of her nose that she felt earlier had become a full-blown headache spreading throbbing pain from her temples to the back of her head. She took slow, deep breaths to try and relax before the pain became worse. Wanda slowed the van to a crawl. The police car looked out of place parked in front of the two-story stucco house.

"Who cares about the police car?" Wanda said, as she brought the van closer to the house. "Look who just walked out the door."

Holly opened her eyes and watched as a Fulton County policeman and her client, Michael Williams, left the house. From the way Michael was clutching the piece of paper in his hand, he might be a former client. He got another fine, she thought, as the van came to a halt.

"He doesn't look happy to see us," said Wanda.

Holly grabbed the handle of the door and stepped out of the van. "It's my job to make him happy." She opened the door as the policeman drove away.

She'd met many handsome men while her father had campaigned for office. Some were handsome in a scholarly way, some were even downright pretty, but Michael Williams was handsome in a blatantly masculine way. The photographs didn't convey the full extent of his appeal. Sensuality surrounded him like the haze on a hot summer morning. A plain white cotton T-shirt stretched over his wide, muscular shoulders. Old, faded blue jeans molded to his lean hips. He stood with his legs apart and his thumbs thrust through the empty belt loops of his jeans. Tall, dark, and dangerous— the phrase fit him.

His thick black hair was cut short, in an almost military style. His face was a study in contrasts. His brown cheeks were high and angular, his chin strong and square. Thick straight brows were perfectly formed over his dark brown-black eyes. As she walked toward him, she felt like a lamb entering the territory of an indulgent predator, never quite knowing when the predator would strike.

"Mr. Williams?" Holly held out her hand. "I'm Holly Aimes with Security Force." Good grief, he's tall, she thought, as she stood in front of him. At five-ten, she rarely had to look up to a man but she had to look up at him.

He slowly reached out and took her outstretched hand. As his rough, calloused fingers touched hers, an unwelcome ripple of desire spread through her body like a pebble dropped into a calm pond. *What's wrong with you, Holly? This man is a customer. Now isn't the time to let emotions override common sense!* Holly straightened her shoulders in an attempt to dismiss the renegade emotion that had caught her totally off guard. She met his gaze. For a brief moment, she saw a flicker of undefinable emotion in his eyes; then it was gone. Abruptly she released his hand.

"Miss Aimes, do you know why the police were here?" His voice was low and deep, with just a hint of a West Coast accent. "Let me tell you why. You see this?" He held out the paper. "This is a fine, and I've got another one that looks exactly like it. Would you like to guess why I have them?"

"Mr. . . ." she began, her voice husky. She cleared her throat and fought to keep any hint of her wayward emotion from showing. "Mr. Williams, Security Force will pay the fines. If you give me the tickets, I'll have a check made out for them tomorrow." She hoped he didn't notice the slight trembling of her hand when he gave her the ticket.

"I'm glad your company's doing that . . ."

Holly breathed a sigh of relief when Wanda approached them carrying a large tool kit. The sexual pull between them was like nothing she'd felt before— with a client, or with anyone else. She needed to get things back on a business level. "This is our technician, Wanda Johnson."

Wanda placed the tool kit on the ground and held out her hand. "Hello, Mr. Williams."

"Hello." He shook her hand and turned back to Holly. "Like I said . . . paying the fine is all well and good, but that's not going to stop my alarm from going off every night."

"Why don't you show us what you were doing when it went off?"

Holly followed Wanda and Michael through the open door. The house wasn't what she'd expected. Although she'd been in several houses in this community, the others had had a professional designer's stamp on them. This one didn't. The overstuffed beige sofa looked as if it had been chosen for comfort rather than style. The living room was inviting and had a relaxed air that invited the visitor to make himself at home. Michael led them up a winding oak staircase to the second floor. Holly's gaze slid to the well-worn denim that covered his hips. She had to force herself to look at the back of his head as she climbed the stairs behind him. *What's wrong with you, Holly Aimes? Get your mind back on business.*

"This is where I was when the alarm went off last night." He opened the oak double doors and motioned for them to go inside.

My living room and dining room would fit in the sitting area of his bedroom. Floor-to-ceiling bookshelves lined the walls. The last remaining sunlight filtered through the large picture windows, spreading a golden glow across the room.

Michael walked to the alarm panel on the wall. "I set the alarm here and walked across the hall to my office, and as soon as I set foot into the room, the alarm went off." The right side of his mouth lifted in a gesture of disgust. "I *specifically* asked that my office be accessible during the night. I know I had my business manager add it to your contract."

"Mr. Williams, you're right. Accessibility to your office *was* written in your contract. If you'll let us look at your system, I'm sure we'll find out what's activating the alarm and fix the problem."

"You've got this one last time, Ms. Aimes." He looked directly into her eyes and held her gaze for a long, tense moment, then walked out of his bedroom and down the stairs. Holly relaxed her tense shoulders. Why did she feel as if she had just walked safely out of the den of an angry lion?

Two

Michael sat at the pine dinette table in the breakfast area. Four movie scripts lay untouched on the table in front of him. One of the scripts might be the one that could change his career from talk-show host to movie producer. His move from his hometown of Los Angeles to Atlanta had certainly been a step in the right direction. Tod Thomas, renegade television mogul, had offered him more money and complete control of his show if he'd switch from his old network to Thomas Broadcast System. Michael left his old network. He and the executive producers had had too many disagreements about the format of the show, and he wasn't happy with the offer they'd made for his new contract.

Michael drank the last of his soft drink and tossed the can toward the recycle bin across the room. He missed. Michael picked up the can and placed it in the container.

He surveyed his favorite room in the house, the kitchen, and he smiled in satisfaction. The room was exactly like he wanted it. Bright, shiny appliances of all kinds lined the ample counter space, and copper-bottomed pots and pans hung from the ceiling over the island. Windows surrounded the room. He had all the space he needed when he wanted to cook.

Never mind that he ruined everything he tried to cook; it was the process that counted. Besides, he needed to learn how to cook. He had a feeling that his chef, Amy Tanner, wasn't going to last. For lunch, she had served tofu spread and wheat germ bread when he'd asked for a ham sandwich.

Amy was the third chef he'd had since moving to Atlanta four months before. The first had taken pictures of the interior of his house and sold them to a tabloid, the second had thought she should do her cooking in his bedroom as well as the kitchen, and Amy . . . well, she was fine when she started to work for him. She submitted menus for his approval one week in advance and the food was excellent. For dinner, she'd prepare a seven-course meal or sloppy joes if he asked her. She was a great chef until she'd joined some new-age organization. Now, he had to guess the ingredients of his meals. He didn't want to even *think* about what she'd prepared for dinner tonight. Whatever it was, it was green and he didn't recognize it.

With a sigh, he walked back to the dinette table and sat down. He knew he should be working, but he kept thinking of Holly Aimes. *Striking:* that was the word that came to mind. She wasn't beautiful in the classic sense of the word. He was accustomed to having beautiful women around him. In Los Angeles, anyone could become beautiful for the right price and with a good plastic surgeon.

Her features were too exotic, too mysterious to be considered pretty. Pretty was too tame. She had rich, warm brown skin that looked smooth and soft, and a mouth that was a little too wide for her face. High, delicate cheeks and chin accented her oval face, but it was her dark brown eyes that made him want to discover what lay behind the ice maiden facade. He had been a talk-show host long enough to recognize when someone was hiding something. The cool mask she presented to the world contradicted the brief shimmer of heat in her eyes. Something had happened to this woman that made her want to hide, and that mystery made him take notice.

Her engagement to Trey Christian had made her name and face familiar to him and to everyone else in the entertainment field. The fact that her father was governor of Georgia didn't hurt, either. She was exactly the type of person he liked to have as a guest on his show. Since she hadn't given any interviews, it would be an exclusive, a coup. There was more to Holly Aimes than the cold facade she presented to the world. It would be interesting to discover the real Holly.

Michael rubbed his eyes and leaned back in the dinette chair. She really wasn't his type. He liked women with more meat on their bones. She was slim to the point of skinny, and he liked full, lush women. He looked at his watch to interrupt the lustful thoughts running through his head. Well, Ms. Aimes had better hurry and find the problem. He had other things to do besides wait around for them to finish. Maybe he would try his hand at grilling fish. How hard could that be?

* * *

An hour and forty-five minutes later, Holly and Wanda still didn't know why the system wasn't working properly. "What are we overlooking?" Holly asked in frustration. She had been sitting in Michael's office, working on her laptop computer, for the last thirty minutes. She rubbed her eyes, which were tired from staring at the computer drawing of Michael's house. She had checked and rechecked her information and still couldn't find the problem.

"I don't know, Holly." Wanda rolled out a stack of blue papers onto the solid teakwood desk. They were the final blueprints. She flipped the pages until she came to the second-story floor plan. "We've checked every piece of equipment in the house and everything works like it's supposed to." Wanda pointed to the page. "There's no reason for the thing not to work."

Holly rose out of the soft leather executive chair and stood beside Wanda. Time was running out. Michael had stayed out of their way while they'd worked, but Holly knew with each passing minute, their chances of finding the problem grew slimmer.

"Wait a minute," Holly said. She looked from her computer to the blueprints. "They aren't the same."

"What?" Wanda leaned over to look at the two drawings. "Of course, they're the same."

"No. Look at the dimensions."

Wanda glanced from one drawing to another. "You're right. They aren't the same. I wonder which one is correct?"

"There's only one way to find out. Where's the tape measure?"

Minutes later, Holly made revisions on her computer. "I can't believe that he made changes and didn't let us know. The idiot!"

"The customer, Holly, the customer."

"The customer is an idiot."

Wanda laughed. "We're going to have to tell him that we can't fix his system tonight."

"Yeah. That'll be a thrill." Holly typed the last of the commands and turned off her laptop. "Let's pack up everything before I go downstairs and talk to the idi . . . I mean, customer."

Michael looked at the smoky black mass that had once been a filet of fish. The cookbook sitting to the right of his indoor grill made grilling sound so easy. He had followed the directions, well, most of the directions, to the letter. Instead of grilled trout, he had blackened matter. The hum of the overhead exhaust fan drowned out the sizzle of the hot fish. With stainless steel tongs, he removed the trout from the grill and placed it on the plate along with three other blackened masses. He stared at the plate in disgust and threw the tongs down beside it.

Cooking wasn't hard. He'd heard that from his parents, his two brothers, and various girlfriends when they'd tried to show him how to cook. If cooking was so easy, why couldn't he do it?

He went to the refrigerator door, where a list of restaurants that delivered was held up by a sandwich-shaped magnet, and snatched the phone off the hook. He had just dialed the number to a Chinese restaurant when Holly and Wanda entered.

Holly gave him a brief smile before she spotted the plate full of burnt fish. He could tell by the puzzled expression on her face and the crinkling of her nose that the exhaust fan hadn't totally cleared the charred smell from the kitchen. I should have hidden the plate in the refrigerator, he thought.

He motioned for them to have a seat at the dinette table, placed his order for Chinese food, and joined them.

"Mr. Williams," Holly said. "There seems to be a problem. The floor plan that we have and the actual layout of the house don't match." She placed a sheet of blue paper in front of him and pointed to an area on the second floor. "The size of your office and the hallway leading to the bedroom don't match the plans that we have."

Michael could smell the light, floral scent of her perfume along with the faint smell of burnt fish as he looked at the blueprint. For a few seconds, he savored Holly's sweet smell. It sent sharp yearnings to his belly. It had been a long time since he'd been this deeply attracted to a woman. Get with the program, Williams, he thought, irritated with himself. He concentrated on the floor plan in front of him.

"You're right," he said. "This isn't the same. I had the architect change the plan to get more office space."

"Mr. Williams, did you or the architect contact Security Force when you decided to change the floor plan?"

"No." Michael watched as Wanda and Holly exchanged looks.

Wanda looked down at her folded hands and Holly picked up the paper and rolled it into a tube. He thought for a moment that she was going to hit him with it.

"Your alarm system doesn't work because you changed the floor plans." Holly began tapping the paper against the table. "When we put together your system, we designed it using the lengths and dimensions you provided. We assumed that the information was correct."

"I didn't think that lengthening a wall would affect the alarm system." Michael laughed mockingly. "I didn't really think about the alarm system at all." He paused and said, "Your people were over here before. Why didn't they find the problem then?"

"Unless my employees measured the wall, they wouldn't know that you changed the length," she said sharply. "It was in our contract that if you made any changes in the design of your house, you would notify us. We can't guarantee that the system will work without your cooperation."

"Miss Aimes, the wall was only moved a foot." He shrugged his shoulders. "What difference does it make?"

"It's obviously the difference between your alarm working and not working." She placed the blueprint on the table. "Did you make any other changes?"

"No."

"We'll have to replace some equipment in the hall and in your office."

Michael looked at his watch. "How long will it take?"

"An hour, hour and a half." Holly looked at Wanda for confirmation and Wanda nodded. "The only problem is we don't have the equipment on our truck. We'll have to return later to complete the job."

"Great. That's just great." He leaned back in his chair with his arms folded across his chest. His annoyance was evident in his tone.

Holly interrupted, "What time should we arrive tomorrow?"

"You might as well come over early and get it over with. How about ten?"

"We'll be here."

"We've got Bobby and Whitney scheduled for next Thursday." Andy Kurtz shuffled through his appointment book, which lay open on the soft couch in Michael's living room. Andy conducted himself as if he were wearing a business suit and not a denim shirt and tan Dockers. His attention to detail was reflected in the highly polished gleam of his round, dark-rimmed glasses and the high gloss shine of his burgundy loafers. He was a short, wiry man who could get things done.

Michael put his feet, clad in old, scuffed basketball shoes, on the coffee table and glanced down at the schedule of guests to appear on his show. The bright morning sun filtered through the large windows in his living room.

"Good. What about Halle? Have we gotten a firm

date from her office?'' Michael continued speaking without giving his assistant a chance to reply. ''Call the public relations office of the Braves, the Hawks and the Falcons. See if we can get someone from each team to talk about sports here in Atlanta.'' He put aside the schedule and glanced up at Andy. ''Get all the information on Holly Aimes as soon as possible.''

''Holly Aimes,'' Andy said thoughtfully. ''Oh, you mean Trey Christian's old fiancée. Are you going to invite her to be on the show?''

''Maybe,'' Michael said evasively.

''I don't think she's given an interview herself. Usually Trey or a member of her family talks to the press.'' Andy tapped his pen on his appointment book, his lips pursed in concentration. ''If she doesn't want to be on the show, it might be interesting to invite her brother, Robert. He and Trey are appearing in the same movie next month.'' Andy leaned forward, ''I think people would like to know his side of the story, since he introduced Trey and Holly.''

''Let's wait. I want to see what kind of information you get on Holly first.''

Andy wrote in his appointment book. ''I'll see what I can find out.''

''Great.'' Michael closed his eyes. He had been up since seven o'clock, which would have been like three o'clock in the morning for anyone else. His normal working hours were from four in the afternoon until two or three in the morning, but today he wanted to make sure he was awake and alert when Holly arrived at his house. So far, he had only managed to be awake.

Michael forced his eyes open and removed his feet from the table. "Okay, let's look at the sweeps week lineup." There wasn't any part of the production of his show that he didn't get involved with. It wasn't that he didn't trust the people doing the job, it was just in his nature to be a workaholic. The three Emmys on his bookshelf were a testament to his work. Also, he got bored doing the same thing.

Over the years, his show had changed its format at least four times so his audience never knew what to expect. Surprise guests ranged from Michael Jackson to the President of the United States. The viewers loved it. His show was always rated number one in its time slot.

Michael and Andy were engrossed in their work when the doorbell rang. Michael looked at his watch. It was five to ten.

"Good morning, Mr. Williams," Holly said, her voice smooth with a slight southern accent. The khaki jumpsuit she wore clung to her small, pert breasts before draping down to her slim waist and long, long legs.

" 'Morning. Come on in." He stepped aside to let them enter before closing his front door. He wanted her. That hadn't changed in the twelve hours since he'd last seen her.

"This is my assistant, Andy Kurtz." Michael motioned to Andy, who rose from the large, overstuffed sofa and acknowledged her presence. "We'll be here in the living room, out of your way."

"Fine," Holly said.

Michael watched as Holly and Wanda walked down the hall and up the stairs. He still didn't understand what was so bad about the change in the floor plan, but it had given him another chance to have Holly in his house.

He rejoined the waiting Andy, who was polishing his already clean glasses with a white handkerchief. "I didn't make the connection between Holly Aimes and the company that put in your alarm system." Andy folded the handkerchief in a neat square before returning it to his pants pocket. "I'm surprised she came out here with the technician."

"I told her to take out the security system if they couldn't fix it. I guess she wanted to make sure the job was done right."

"Oh," Andy nodded his head. "Have you found out anything about her former fiancé?"

"No." Michael sat down on the sofa. "But I will."

A few minutes later, Andy closed his briefcase and stood. "I'll double-check everything when I get back to the studio." Andy paused when he heard someone walking down the stairs. When no one appeared in the living room, he said, "I'll also start looking for information on the other."

Michael nodded. He understood that Andy was referring to Holly Aimes. He followed his assistant to the front door. "I'll see you later, Andy." It was only ten-thirty in the morning, but the heat and humidity made it feel as if it were afternoon. He stepped back into his cool, air-conditioned home. He and Andy had accomplished more than he'd expected this morning, he thought, as he walked to his kitchen.

He paused when he saw Wanda standing in the utility area. He had forgotten that someone had come downstairs while he and Andy were talking.

"Hi," he said. "Is it all right if I get something to drink?"

"Oh, yeah. It's okay to move around the house. We've turned off the system until we add the other equipment." She continued to work on the metal box.

She looks like a pixie, he thought, grasping a can of soda from the refrigerator.

She caught him looking at her and gave a cautious smile.

"Will it bother you if I ask a question?" he asked, straddling a chair before he sat down.

"Uh, no."

"Why won't the alarm work the way it is?"

Wanda was silent for a few seconds. She continued to work on the box before speaking. "When you moved the wall back a foot, the motion detector at the end of the hall would pick up your movements when you entered your office. If the wall had remained where it was . . ." She paused when Holly walked into the room. "I was explaining to Mr. Williams why his alarm system didn't work."

"Please go ahead," Holly said.

Why do I feel like I've been called to the principal's office? Michael thought, glancing from one to the other.

"As I was saying, if the wall had remained where it was, it would have blocked the beam and the motion detector wouldn't have picked up your movements."

Embarrassed, he stared down at the can of soda. He hoped that he didn't look as uncomfortable as he felt. "What happened when the other technicians came over? Why didn't they find the problem?"

"If somebody looked at the floor plan, they probably didn't think to measure the walls to see if they were the right length," Wanda said. "They didn't have the correct information, so they looked for problems in the equipment and wiring, not structural problems."

He felt as if he had dug himself into a hole and couldn't get out. He sat in silence, searching for a way to backpedal.

"Wanda, I've put in the equipment upstairs. Are you finished down here?"

"Yep."

"I'll go back upstairs and test it."

Michael watched her walk out of the kitchen. Her jumpsuit couldn't hide the soft sway of her hips. He glanced down at the can of soda. "I guess I really messed up by not giving you guys the correct information."

"You sure did," she said.

A series of beeps came from the box where Wanda had been working. Seconds later, another beep sounded. Michael figured he should let her finish her work. He rose and walked out of the kitchen. He had done enough damage already.

"Well, that should take care of it, Mr. Williams," Holly said, as she walked into the living room.

"Listen, I apologize again for not letting your

company know about the changes in the floor plan." He had managed to put both feet in his mouth and he hoped he could salvage the situation.

"Apology accepted," she said, though she didn't look like she accepted it. "We rewired the hall and your office. Your system is working fine now. No problem."

"No. I should have asked the architect to call you and tell you about the room switch." Michael ran his hand over his hair. "Let me make it up to you and . . . ?" He turned to Wanda.

"Wanda. Wanda Johnson," she answered with a smile.

"Let me take you and Wanda to lunch. That'll be my way of apologizing."

"No, that won't be necessary. We're just doing our job," Holly said.

"You're not just doing your job. I've caused you unnecessary trips to my house and a long drive back to your office."

"We're accustomed to it. We do this for a living." Holly turned to Wanda and asked, "Are you ready?"

"The van's all packed up. Goodbye, Mr. Williams."

"Call me Mike, Wanda."

Wanda smiled shyly at him.

"Goodbye," Holly said, and walked out of the living room.

Michael escorted them to the front door. He watched as they climbed into their van.

"Now, let me get this straight." Pam leaned back in the chair and folded her arms across her chest.

"Michael Williams, *the* Michael Williams, who has a top-rated talk show, asked you to go out to lunch with him?"

"Well, he actually invited Wanda and me to lunch." Holly flipped through the mail on her desk. Pam had come to her office within minutes after she had arrived back at the office. Holly had the feeling that Pam had asked the receptionist to keep an eye out for her return.

"And you said no."

"Yes," she said, placing the letter she'd been reading on her desk. Holly looked up at Pam. She had that "I smell something foul" look on her face.

"You're out of your mind." She looked up at the ceiling, her hands uplifted. "I work with a crazy woman," she said, as if she were speaking to the Almighty.

Holly squirmed in her chair when Pam stared at her incredulously. "Pam, please."

"Please. Now, there's a good word. Please, I would love to go out to lunch with you. Please, take me to lunch. Please, just take me." Pam shook her head. "You had the chance that hundreds, maybe thousands, of black women all over the United States would die, kill, give up chocolate for, and you turned him down?"

"He's a client." She picked up the letter she'd set aside earlier and began reading it, hoping that Pam would drop the subject. She didn't think Pam would take the hint, but she could always hope.

Pam plucked the letter out of her hands and slapped it on her desk. "We own the company, Holly. We can make up the rules as we go. If Blair

Underwood was our client and he asked me to lunch . . ." Pam stood up from the chair and put her hands on her hips. "Yes would be out of my mouth so fast, he wouldn't know what hit him."

"He's a client, that's all."

"That's not what Wanda said."

"Wanda?" Holly sat straighter in her chair.

"She said that he was very interested in you."

Holly rolled her eyes. "Wanda doesn't know what she's taking about. Mr. Williams was just happy to get his alarm system fixed. He was probably happy to get us out of his house."

"You think so?"

"Yes. Besides, the last thing I need is to have the press think I'm going out with another famous person. Trey Christian was enough for me. Remember him?"

"How could I forget?" Pam's voice rose an octave. "The man broke your heart, damn his hide. Then left *you* to deal with the press after he got married. We never had so many reporters come to the office." She sat again in the chair she had vacated and smiled. "Robyn made their life miserable when they walked in the door."

Holly smiled, remembering the competent way their receptionist, Robyn, had handled the press. Her smile slowly died as she also remembered the phone calls to her home and the television crews parked in front of the office. All of that publicity over a broken engagement. No . . . she wouldn't go through that again.

"I was really glad when he came back from his

honeymoon. That got me off the hook for a while when the press went after him."

"Ha!"

Holly ignored Pam's sarcastic remark. "I couldn't begin to imagine what would happen if Michael Williams and I were seen together." She shuddered just thinking about it.

"I'd imagine he'd take you to a romantic dinner or a play."

"Reporters yelling questions, photographers taking pictures."

Pam scowled at her. "Afterward, he'd take you home, ask you for another date, and kiss you goodnight."

"Come back, Pam. Come back to reality."

"Are you telling me you didn't feel *any* sort of sexual attraction to Michael Williams?"

"No, I didn't," Holly said quickly, then remembered how she'd felt when she'd seen him standing in front of his house when they'd first met. The raw chemistry had been a little overwhelming. He'd made her feel sensual with just a glance. She'd just as soon keep that little tidbit of information to herself. Michael Williams was a client, and that was that.

"Oh, well. Maybe *I'll* get a chance to meet him." Pam said, watching her partner intently from beneath her lowered eyelids. "Who knows, maybe he'll ask me out."

"What happened to Steve? I thought you were dating him."

"Steve and I are just friends," Pam said.

"Holly?" Robyn, their receptionist, stood at the

door holding a gift-wrapped box. "There's a package for you." She walked over and placed the box on the desk.

Holly studied it. "Did it have a note attached?"

"No." Robyn shrugged her shoulders. "This is the way it came."

"Hurry up and open the thing, Holly," Pam said, moving to the edge of her chair.

Holly tore the paper from the box and frowned in confusion at the FAO Schwartz name on the box inside. She lifted the top and two helium balloons floated to the ceiling. Holly smiled and lifted out a teddy bear with a sad expression on its face. A card was taped to its hand. *I would be very sad if you didn't have lunch with me— Michael.*

"Who's it from?" Pam asked, walking around to read the note.

Holly picked up the bear and gave Pam the note. Pam read it and put it down on the desk.

"He was so glad to get you out of the house, he sent you a teddy bear," Pam said, in a sickeningly sweet voice.

Holly stroked the soft fur of the stuffed animal. That was really nice, she thought. In all the time she had dated Trey, he'd never sent her a teddy bear. He had sent her the traditional red rose. In retrospect, she realized that Trey wasn't ever very original.

Get a grip, Holly. You just said that Michael Williams was off limits. She put the bear back into the box and closed the top over it.

"Don't tell me you're going to send it back."

"All right, I won't tell you."

"Holly, don't be stupid! The man is obviously interested in you. Why don't you take advantage of it?"

Holly looked at Robyn, who was trying to leave the room unnoticed. "Thanks for bringing me the box." She waited until the door to her office was closed before turning back to Pam.

"Back off, Pam."

"Back off. Back off. I backed off when you got engaged to that sleazy Trey Christian, and look what happened."

"I'm serious, Pam. Stay out of this."

They glared at each other until Pam looked away.

"Okay, Holly, have it your way."

Three

Holly dreaded going to her father's latest political campaign dinner-dance. She had attended so many that they all seemed the same. A boring meal of dry chicken and bland vegetables served on fine china, a mediocre band playing, and her father giving a speech. Money was never mentioned, but guests were always expected to make a contribution.

The same type of people always attended: people with power, like her father; people who wanted power, like his campaign manager; and people who wanted to be seen with the people with power— the political groupies.

Holly entered the lobby of the Doubleday Hotel. Her black evening gown was the latest gift that her stepmother had delivered to her office. Jean Aimes always called the gowns gifts, but Holly knew that this was Jean's way of making sure Holly wasn't photographed wearing the same outfit too often. Holly could almost hear her say, "It would be bad for your father's image." She'd heard that phrase time and time again during her childhood and adolescence.

Holly entered an empty elevator and pressed the button to the lower lobby. Polished mirrors lined the elevator walls from floor to ceiling. She studied her image and carefully checked her appearance. The gown's scoop neckline accented her small breasts. If Pam wore this dress, she'd look elegant. I look like Olive Oyl, she thought. The black gown hugged her slim waist and curved hips without being obvious. The long skirt made her look taller. The memory of the quarter-page picture on the *Atlanta Journal*'s society page with her dressed to the nines and her bra strap showing still embarrassed her. Not a bra strap in sight, she thought. She ran her hand over her hair. The trip to the hairdresser earlier this afternoon helped control her straightened bangs and blunt shoulder-length hair; otherwise the heat and humidity would have made her hair impossible to manage.

The doors of the elevators opened and she entered the lobby. Two women in tasteful evening gowns smiled at Holly as she walked past them. Her stepmother, Jean, would have stopped and talked to them because they were the wives of the mayor and the lieutenant governor, but Holly didn't want to talk to anyone tonight.

She was still upset about the argument she and Pam had had this afternoon. Over the years, they'd had disagreements, but none so disturbing as this one. Holly wasn't going to think about their argument tonight. There were only a few more appearances to make with her family before election day; then she wouldn't attend another event . . . ever. Instead of becoming accustomed to attending these events, as her stepmother Jean had suggested, Holly grew more uncomfortable in the public eye, until she couldn't stand the idea of going through another political campaign with her family.

She opened one of the curved double doors at the end of the lobby. The smell of expensive perfume blended with the smell of baked chicken in the adjoining dining hall. Her father and stepmother were mingling in the front of the room with the mayor and members of his staff. Holly walked through the maze of people wearing designer gowns and custom-made tuxedos.

She heard bits of conversation over the noisy crowd. The rise in the crime rate and the last pay increase voted in by the Senate were some of the subjects she heard as she made her way through the crowd. She spotted her younger sister and brother from across the room. Sandra and Robert, Jr., were talking with her paternal grandmother and two federal court judges. Holly joined them and accepted a glass of wine from one of the waiters who moved smoothly among the guests. Her grandmother directed the conversation so that the judges were now talking with Sandra and she maneuvered Holly away from the others.

Seventy-six years old, Nola Hollbrook Aimes used her age and frail appearance to browbeat her family until she got her way. At five foot and one hundred pounds, she still had the grace and style that had made her popular with the political crowd. More than one young politician thought Nola Aimes was a sweet old lady until her sharp mind and even sharper tongue caused him to give her respect.

"What do you think of my new outfit, Holly? Nice, isn't it?"

"Yes, it's very nice, Grandma."

"Jean sent over an ugly gray dress that she wanted me to wear tonight, but I went to Neiman Marcus and exchanged it for this." The brilliant royal blue dress with a matching beaded jacket would have looked ridiculous on another woman Nola's age, but Nola still had style and could carry it off. Her short, thick gray hair was cut in a simple but elegant style. She looked at Holly's gown. "Did Jean choose that dress for you?" At Holly's nod, she said, "It figures. She buys a beautiful dress for you and she sends me a dress that I wouldn't be caught dead in. I swear, Jean must think I'm old." She glanced at her watch. "You were almost late." She paused and smiled at the mayor when he walked past them. "Stupid fool. I'm surprised he's still in office," she muttered, and turned back to Holly. "You know how Jean gets about these 'appearances.' You'd think the whole election depended on whether or not you showed up for these things." Her grandmother brushed a nonexistent speck of lint off of her jacket.

"I know." Holly took a sip of wine. "I almost decided to pretend to be sick, but then I remembered that the last time I did that, she came over afterward with medicine."

"Hmm, I'll have to remember that one. Well, we won't have to deal with this much longer."

"No, it won't be long now."

"Won't be long for what?" Her brother joined them. Robert had inherited their father's height and good looks. He'd cut his thick, curly black hair for a part in an upcoming movie. His high cheekbones and smooth reddish-brown skin had been inherited from a distant paternal Native American ancestor. From his mother, he'd inherited light amber eyes. His tuxedo hid his muscular build, but it was his boy-next-door face and his outgoing personality that made him stand out in the crowd— as well as on the movie screen.

"Well, look who's decided to join us," Grandma Aimes said. "That young woman read you right, Junior." Her brother groaned at the pet name. "You're just a flirt, and you know it."

"If I didn't flirt, Grandma, you'd think there was something wrong with me."

"Uh-huh."

"Don't try and change the subject." Robert placed a hand on Nola's shoulder. "What are you and Holly up to?"

Nola hesitated, then looked around the room to see if anyone was close enough to overhear their conversation. She stepped closer to her grandchildren. "Holly and I are counting down the days until the elections are over; then we can get on with our lives." Nola Aimes motioned for one of the waiters. "And I'll get some decent food."

Holly and Robert laughed. Food was Grandma Aimes's weakness. She liked all kinds of food— except "banquet" food, as she called it. "I'm glad the production of the movie is over," Robert said woefully. "Pascal's Restaurant catered for us, and I ate too much good southern food."

"If I'd known that Pascal's was serving the food,

I'd have come to see you on location more often," Nola said.

"Right, Grandma," he said mockingly. "You didn't want to put up with Trey." His voice trailed off suddenly and he flashed Holly a guilty look. "I'm sorry."

"It's okay," she said softly. "Trey doesn't matter to me anymore."

Nola shook her head before Robert could speak again. "So, when are you going to take me out to dinner again, Junior?"

Holly could tell that they didn't realize that Trey couldn't hurt her now. They'll learn, she thought to herself. She listened as her grandmother and brother discussed a new restaurant that had opened in midtown when a flash of light nearly blinded her. She had noticed the photographers when she'd come in but had lost track of them when she'd reached her grandmother. She turned her head in the opposite direction of the light. From experience, she knew that photographers were always ready to take a second picture when the person looked toward the flash of light. Damn those reporters. I can't wait to get away from all of this, she thought and glanced at her watch.

Five more minutes before dinner was to be served. Then, the television cameramen and newspaper photographers would turn their attention exclusively to her father, which was exactly where she wanted their attention to stay. Holly didn't like the fishbowl existence her life had become over the last four years. As the voters of Georgia began demanding tougher enforcement of ethics laws, political mud-slinging had become the occupation of choice among candidates.

When official after official was found guilty of wrongdoing, her father had become the golden example of the Senate. With his spotless record and charismatic personality, he became a symbol of what politicians were supposed to be, and the public couldn't get enough information about him or his family.

"Well, well, well." Robert looked toward the doors. "Dad said he had a surprise, but I didn't expect this." Holly followed her brother's glance.

Michael Williams stood just beyond the doors.

Camera lights and flash units illuminated him as reporters and other guests moved toward him. His broad shoulders were accentuated by his black tuxedo jacket. He seemed totally at ease as the center of attention.

He glanced up suddenly and looked directly at her. For a moment, she felt as if he could see through to her very being, as if all her defenses lay useless on the ground and Michael Williams could see the real her. *Run!* her mind told her. He held her gaze and she felt the danger of his presence like prey just before the predator moved in for the kill. Immediately, the room seemed warmer and the air a little heavier. A sense of anticipation spread through her body. This is stupid, she told herself, and looked down at her wineglass.

She had been around handsome men before and hadn't felt the attraction she felt for Michael. She took a sip of wine and told herself to ignore him, but she found herself looking in his direction. Her hands tightened around the glass when he left the group and moved in her direction. He walked with an easy, sexy stride that made many heads turn as he moved through the room. Occasionally, he paused to speak with another person, but he never lost sight of his goal.

Holly vaguely heard her grandmother call her name but she couldn't take her gaze from Michael. Tall, handsome, and very, very dangerous. Yes, danger was what she felt when he was near.

"Hello, Holly." Michael stood in front of her.

Even in her high heels, she had to tilt her head to look into his face. He was the perfect height for embracing. Where did that come from, she wondered. "What are you doing here?" she asked coolly.

"Holly Aimes, you mind your manners." Her grandmother gave her a stern look, then smiled graciously at Michael. "I'm Nola Aimes. Robert Aimes is my son. These are my grandchildren, Robert, Jr., and Sandra. I take it that you and Holly know each other?"

"Yes, Holly's company put in the alarm system in my house, Ms. Aimes. I'm Michael Williams."

"It's nice to meet you, young man." Her pleasant smile melted and irritation took its place. "Oh, Lord, here comes that big mouth . . ."

Holly almost groaned aloud when she saw Ms. Banks heading toward them. Despite her small stature, Anna Banks had the biggest mouth and the sharpest tongue in Atlanta.

"Why, Anna, good to see you," her grandmother said, as she joined Ms. Banks, giving the rest of the group time to escape.

Michael took Holly's arm and led them away. "Your grandmother is smooth."

"Yes, she is. What *are* you doing here? I saw the guest list last night and you weren't on it." Her voice was full of suspicion.

"I'm here to see you," he said, in a soft, sexy voice.

She looked at him in disbelief. "You're here to see *me?*"

"Yes. I believe in the 'If at first you don't succeed, keep asking and eventually she'll say yes' policy."

"Oh, please."

"It's true. The more you hang around and keep asking, the more the chance of a yes increases. I intend to get a yes from you."

"You're wasting your time and mine. I don't go out with my clients."

In the crowded room, an uneasy silence surrounded them. With her chin tilted, she looked into his eyes, determined to stand her ground. Then, as if a curtain had been lifted, the congenial talk-show host was gone and in his place was a dark, seductively dangerous man. "Our business relationship will come to an end sooner or later. I won't always be your client." Holly felt a shiver of apprehension. Before she could respond, the congenial talk-show host was back. "We don't have to go out. We'll just be two people who happen to do business, who happen to be in the same place at the same time, who happen to be sitting next to each other, who happen to be eating at the same time. While one person (that's me) apologizes to the other person (that's you). Dating will never be mentioned. I won't ask you to go out with me."

Yet.

The word hung between them. Had she imagined the change in him? She studied the man standing before her. His expression was unassuming and candid. She must be imagining things. Besides, there was no way she was going to get involved with him . . . a man like her father and ex-fiancé who thrived in the spotlight. She was too close to getting out of the spotlight to let her plans be swayed by him. "Have you been to a political dinner before?"

He raised his eyebrows. "I take it you're not going for the idea?"

"No."

The five-piece band played a sad rendition of a classic hit from tho fifties. Holly wondered how much time she had before she could leave. Dinner had consisted of dry chicken breast with peach sauce, undercooked green beans with almonds, and for dessert, something that resembled a cup of Pepto Bismol.

Her father had given his speech, and now was the time she hated most: dancing. So far, she had danced with her father, her brother, and various members of her father's staff. She felt like the time was dragging along. She was relieved when the song came to an end. The aide who had been her dancing partner seemed just as happy to end the dance as she was. Maybe she could slip away before anyone else noticed her.

She edged her way to the back of the ballroom. "Leaving so soon, Holly?"

The unmistakable voice of Michael Williams stopped her cold. Damn! Holly slowly turned around. "Yes, I'm leaving." The band began playing the slow jazzy Duke Ellington tune "Satin Doll."

"How about a dance before you leave?" He held out his hand.

She was about to refuse when she spotted a photographer poised to take their picture. Just what I need, Holly thought, as she reluctantly took his hand for the dance.

His hand felt warm and rough. It wasn't the hand of a desk jockey but a hand that had been subjected to hard physical work. As he led her back into the crowd of dancers, she thought, I'll dance this one dance with him, and then I'm leaving. That thought quickly vanished when he took her into his arms.

His heat seemed to surround her like the warmth of a dry sauna. The touch of his hand at her waist seemed to penetrate the fabric of her gown. She kept her gaze on one small button of his white shirt. Instinctively, she knew that it was safer to look at the button than to look at his face. He held her a touch closer than was acceptable, just close enough that she was very aware of their bodies touching but with enough distance that she couldn't really object. He didn't wear cologne, but his unmistakable masculine scent enveloped her senses. They danced in silence, but her body spoke to his in a wordless language.

"Holly," he murmured, when the song came to an end.

She looked into his intense dark brown eyes and she knew that she couldn't lie to herself. She wanted Michael Williams.

"Somebody actually told me "no" today." Michael focused on one member of the audience. If he could keep one person laughing, then he knew his monologue was working. "Like that little word is supposed to stop me." He moved closer to the man on the second level.

Lights beamed down on him from all directions, momentarily blinding him, but he continued to walk toward the audience. He knew every inch of the set and he knew exactly when to stop walking. He made eye contact with several people. He was tempted to concentrate on the group of college students to the right of the set, but the businessman on the second level presented a challenge.

It was his job to make sure that six times a week he made the people in the audience and the television viewers feel like he was having a private conversation with them. He had to make them feel like they were in on a private joke.

"I hate when people tell me no. I get a real bad attitude when they do that." He saw the light on top of one of the cameras turn on and he instinctively moved so that the cameraman could make his shot without ever losing the bond between him and the audience. "It makes me want to do just what they say I can't do." A member of the audience applauded and shouted, "Yeah."

He pointed toward the man. "He knows what I'm

talking about." He turned back to the camera. "I remember when I asked my mama if I could go to this party. It wasn't the party to beat all parties and the only reason I wanted to go was because my older brother got to go. What can I say, I was a teenager." Some members of the audience laughed. "She said I couldn't go. Then I *had* to go to this party. I begged. I pleaded and still she said no. The night of the party I asked her again if I could go. She gave me that 'If you ask me again I'm going to kill you' look. So I decided I was going. I sneaked out the house and walked two blocks to the party. I had a good time. I stayed out two hours past my curfew. It was great . . . until I got home. Everybody in the house, Mama, Daddy, and both my brothers were in my bedroom, waiting for me when I walked in the room. I got the worst punishment of my life that night and that was after Daddy whipped my butt. But . . . I went to the party. So that person that said no to me," Michael looked directly into the lens of the camera, "and you know who you are . . . you're going to say yes. Whether you want to or not." Michael felt a sense of satisfaction when the man laughed. He had connected with the audience and sent a message to a woman who wasn't even there. A woman he was determined to know. She was a challenge, and he didn't pass up challenges.

"Hello, I'm Michael Williams."

The receptionist at the desk of Security Force dropped the pen she was using and stared at him.

Her mouth formed a perfect O. Michael hid his smile. "I'd like to see Holly Aimes, please."

The young woman stared at him for a few seconds. "She . . . she . . . she's not here." She cleared her throat and straightened her shoulders in an attempt to regain her composure. "May I leave a message for her?"

"No. I don't want to leave a message for her. Is her partner here?"

"Yes, Ms. Moore is in. Let me see if she's available." She picked up the phone. "There is a Mr. Michael Williams at the front desk who would like to see Ms. Moore." There was a pause. "Okay, thanks." She hung up the phone. "Ms. Moore will be out in just a minute. Please have a seat."

"Thank you." He paused, then looked at the name plate on the desk, which read "Robyn." He walked to the group of chairs and picked up a copy of *Business Week* . His khaki pants and short-sleeved rugby shirt seemed a bit casual in the office, but his clothes weren't as important as seeing Holly. He stared blindly at the magazine, his mind on Holly Aimes.

In the two days since he had made his threat on his show, he had sent her flowers, a singing telegram, and a box of Godiva chocolates. Nothing had changed her answer. Holly had politely told him, in her soft southern accent, thank you for the gifts, then asked him to stop sending them because she didn't think it was appropriate for them to have dinner together. She had explained that she never mixed business with her personal life.

He didn't know why it was so important to change

her mind. Since he had moved from Los Angeles to Atlanta, he had met several women who were willing to have a casual relationship or more, if he wanted. None had caught his attention like Holly, and businesswise, her appearance on his show would boost his ratings even higher.

She had tried so hard to keep her cool mask in place at the campaign dinner, but he had caught her looking at him when she'd thought he wasn't looking and he'd recognized the longing and desire in her eyes when she'd looked at him. That look had sent a bolt of fire through his body. He'd been relieved when she'd broken out of his arms and hurried from the ballroom. He needed space to understand the attraction he felt for her. Time and space hadn't helped him understand the attraction, but he knew that Holly Aimes was interested in him, and today he would begin a course of action that would tear down her defenses. He would use the very same excuse that she used to keep him at a distance: work.

"Mr. Williams?"

He looked up when he heard his name. Standing in front of him was one of the most beautiful women he had ever seen. She was tall, at least six feet, and had a figure that made a man take notice. She wore a white linen suit with the skirt ending just above her knees, displaying the best set of legs he had seen in a long time. Her hips were softly curved and the belt emphasized her small waist. Everything about her, from her full, high breasts to delicately formed ankles, seemed to exude femininity.

"Mr. Williams, I'm Pam Moore."

"Ms. Moore." His gaze went back to her face. She had the face of an angel, but her eyes revealed her mischievous nature.

"What can I do for you?"

"Well, if we could go to your office, I'd like to discuss something with you." He looked over her shoulder to the receptionist at the desk. Robyn quickly lowered her head.

Pam followed his gaze and smiled. "Yes, right this way."

They walked down the hall to an open door. Sitting on her desk were a spray of roses in every color . . . the roses that he had sent to Holly. She motioned for him to have a seat as she closed the door, then sat behind her desk.

"What can I do for you, Mr. Williams?"

"Mike, please."

"Mike," she nodded her head in acceptance. "Please call me Pam."

"Pam, there seems to be something wrong with my alarm system."

"Oh." She reached for a tablet on her desk. The mischievous expression was gone. Pam was all business. "What's the problem?"

"I don't know. I want somebody from your company to go to the house and check it out."

"Of course, I'll have one of the technicians go out today . . ."

"I don't want just anyone." He held her gaze and watched as her expression changed from confusion to comprehension. He sat quietly in the chair while Pam studied him. He gave an inward sigh of relief

when he saw the faint smile on her face. She would
be an ally.

"Did you have someone in mind, Mike?"

"Yes."

"What would happen if that person couldn't go
to your house and we sent someone else?"

"I'm sure that the problem would get worse and
I would have to call and report the problem." He
paused and folded his arms across his chest, then
said, ". . . every single day."

Pam cleared her throat. "I'm sure that won't happen. However, if anything should happen to hurt
that person, you should know that I will make it my
own personal duty to see that whoever hurt my
friend would regret the day he moved to Atlanta."

He had to admit, the lady was cool. The smile
never left her face, but he knew he had been threatened and she would do her best to carry out her
threat if the situation came about.

"I think I know your position, Pam, and I'll keep
that in mind."

There was a brief knock on the door before it
was opened.

"Pam, do you have— oh. I'm sorry. I didn't mean
to interrupt." Holly stopped abruptly in the office.
She wore a dark gray suit and a prim white shirt.
The color and style of the suit were all wrong for
her, he thought. The short-waisted jacket and long
calf-length skirt made her look extremely tall and
skinny.

"Come in." Pam quickly walked over to Holly and
guided her into the room.

They are like night and day, he thought. Pam was

the fantasy that most men dreamed of, but Holly . . .
Holly had a subtle sexiness if you looked past the
dull clothing.

Mike rose from the chair. "Hello, Holly."

"Mr. Williams. How are you?" She looked at him
with a questioning expression. "Is everything all
right with your alarm system?"

"Yes, the system is fine. Now, you . . . that's a
problem," he said.

"Me?" Holly asked, pointing to herself.

"Yes, you. I have tried and tried to make up for
the trouble I've caused by changing the floor plan
of my house but do I get a chance to do it? No."

"Mr. Williams, you really don't have to do anything," she said crisply.

Her pointed statement made him smile. "Call me
Mike." He continued to speak despite the skeptical
look on her face. "I know I don't have to do anything, but I want to do something. Now, you don't
want to irritate a paying customer, do you? You
know the customer is always right."

"He's got a point, Holly," Pam said, her amusement showing on her face.

"Yeah. I've got a point. Thank you, Pam."

Holly frowned at them both, then looked at Mike
with suspicion. "What do you want, Mike?"

"I would like to take you to dinner. You and the
technician . . ." He raised an eyebrow in question.

"Wanda Johnson," Pam said, and smiled at Holly
and Mike.

"I don't think that's really necessary."

"Why don't we ask Wanda? She might have a different opinion." Mike turned to Pam. "Is she here?"

"Yes, she's just down the hall." Pam walked out the door. Mike smiled at Holly and gestured toward the door. Holly tightened her lips in anger before she turned and walked out of Pam's office. Mike walked behind the two women down the hall to one of the rooms at the end. The room was sectioned off, with office cubicles taking up the majority of space. A small conference table separated a tiny kitchen area. Five people were around it. Coffee cups and manila folders cluttered the surface of the table. The people looked up when they walked in.

"Wanda, you remember Mr. Williams?" **Pam** asked. Wanda blinked once, then twice.

"Hello, Wanda." His voice was deep and masculine.

"Mr. Williams would like for you and Holly to join him for dinner."

"Tonight, if that's okay," Mike asked.

"That sounds great. I'd love to." Wanda saw the frown on Holly's face, then added, "If that's all right with you two."

"Sounds good to me," Pam said, and turned to Holly. "How about it?"

"Well . . . I don't have a problem with Wanda going out to dinner."

"You're included in the invitation, Holly. If there's a problem with dinner tonight, then we can set it up for another time."

"Let me look at my schedule and call you," she said in a cool tone of voice.

"I've got my calendar with me." He held up the burgundy portfolio. "Why don't we check your schedule while I'm here."

He smiled when he saw the irritation in her eyes. *Checkmate.* "As a matter of fact, I'd like to invite your employees to the show Friday night. I'll supply the transportation and backstage passes while we're at dinner." The rest of the employees talked among themselves as the mood of the room changed and an air of anticipation swept through the group.

"I'll have to see how my calendar looks this evening."

Pam, Wanda, and the rest of the employees looked at Holly. There was no mistaking the looks of disbelief on their faces.

"Holly, I'll take over some of your appointments this evening. Go ahead and have dinner. We can take care of the business for a couple hours."

Mike saw the resignation in her eyes. "So where would you two like to go for dinner?" he asked.

Wanda looked at Holly. "Where do you suggest?"

Holly hesitated. "How about the Private Room?"

The Private Room was crowded. Everyone from clerks to powerbrokers dined here. It was also one of the few restaurants that didn't allow the press inside its doors. For that reason, the famous and infamous came here for a quiet meal.

She tried to smooth out the wrinkles in her gray skirt as she stood in front of the doors of the restaurant. She deliberately hadn't changed clothes when she got home. This is a business meal, she told herself, and her suit was perfect for a business meal. Holly had turned down his offer to have a car sent to her house and had insisted on driving herself.

She entered the foyer of the restaurant. Italian marble lined the walls, a black iron railing curved along the second-story balcony, and floral arrangements filled with colorful flowers surrounded the podium, where a tuxedo-clad maitre d' stood.

"May I help you?" he asked.

"No, I'm waiting for someone, thank you." Holly moved to the plush settee next to the wall. She looked at her watch and grimaced. She was just a few minutes early. Hopefully, Wanda would show up soon, she thought, as she looked toward the doors. She felt conspicuous waiting in the foyer.

She wouldn't be here if it weren't for Mike Williams. He had disrupted her thoughts since the night they'd danced together.

As much as she wanted to ignore him, he wouldn't be ignored. She'd found herself reading last month's *Atlanta Magazine* when there was an article about him. She'd stayed up until 12:30 A.M. two nights in a row to watch his program and then scolded herself the next day when she was tired from not getting enough sleep.

Holly looked toward the doors when they opened and felt a tingle of excitement when Mike walked inside. He wore a charcoal-gray suit and a bright red tie. He smiled when he saw her waiting in the foyer.

"Hi," his voice was low, deep, and utterly sexy.

"Hello." Holly cleared her throat. "Did Wanda come with you?"

"No, she said she'd drive here." Mike looked at

his watch. "I'd better let the maitre d' know that we're waiting for our table." He walked to the podium and talked with the man, then went back to Holly.

"Wanda left a message. She can't make it tonight."

"Is this some kind of joke?" She looked at him with suspicion. This sounded fishy.

"No." Mike looked at her, then shrugged his shoulders. "If you don't believe me, you can call her yourself."

"Well." She slowly stood and strapped her purse over her shoulder. "I guess we'd better reschedule this for another time."

"Why? We're here. We might as well eat."

"No, I . . ."

"Holly, why waste the reservation? Give me a chance to apologize."

Holly worried the strap of her purse. She *was* already here. He stepped closer to her. "This is the only time I'll get to eat a decent meal since I fired the chef."

"You fired your chef? What happened?"

"She decided that I needed to eat healthy and started making food like tofu burgers and alfalfa fries."

"Tofu burgers?"

"And alfalfa fries. Fried pieces of green grass."

Holly laughed. "Why didn't you tell her not to cook that stuff?"

"I did. The next day she made meatless tuna salad."

Holly raised her eyebrows. "What's wrong with tuna?"

"I don't know," Mike shook his head. "Tuna wasn't in the stuff that she made, and I didn't eat it."

"It won't take long for you to find a replacement. I'm sure that you can cook your own meals for a couple of days."

"Hmm."

Holly looked at him. "You *do* know how to cook?"

"I can cook . . . sort of."

"Sort of?"

"I can cook a baked potato."

Holly smiled. "That's not cooking."

"So have pity on me and let's eat here."

Holly studied his face for a moment and smiled. "Why not?"

Four

It was too bad that Mike Williams was a really nice man, Holly thought as the waiter served their entrée. Why couldn't he be vain and self-centered? She could resist that type of man. She was having trouble resisting Mike.

For a few moments, they ate in relaxed silence. Then he broke the silence.

"How's your dinner?" he asked.

Holly pressed a white linen napkin to her lips, then answered, "Wonderful. I'll have to order the chicken and penne pasta again." She placed the napkin on her lap and picked up her fork. "How's yours?"

"It tastes great. It has meat in it and I know what it is."

She smiled in amusement. "There's not much you can do to disguise a steak and a baked potato."

"Don't tell that to Amy. She made meatless tuna salad. I wouldn't put it past her to make meatless steak."

Holly laughed at the disgusted look on his face.

"I'm going to have to replace Amy," he said with regret, cutting a piece of his steak. "You don't happen to know a good chef looking for a job?"

"No, but my stepmother, Jean, might be able to help you. Do you want me to get her help?"

"Yes. I don't know how much longer I can handle my own cooking."

Throughout the rest of their dinner, he engaged her in conversation, ranging from the food on the menu to the state of the U.S. economy. They held the conversation to nonpersonal topics. She should have felt at ease with him, but she wasn't. Her heart raced every time she met his dark sensuous gaze. She'd nearly dropped the butter dish when they'd both reached for it during dinner. Her fingers still tingled from his brief but warm touch.

He never once mentioned her previous engagement. People sometimes felt free to ask probing questions about her personal life. Mike didn't ask those types of questions, but what he did ask concerned her.

"We've completed our business dealings, haven't we?" Mike asked, as the waiter served them coffee.

Holly took a careful sip of coffee before answering. "If you mean that you won't see another employee from Security Force in your home, then the answer is yes. Another company monitors your alarm system, so you'll be dealing with them, now that the system is repaired." She looked at him curiously. "Why do you ask?"

"I want to be sure that any contact we have with each other from now on is personal, not business related."

The waiter returned with the receipt and credit card. Mike signed the receipt and placed the card into his wallet. He couldn't have meant it the way it sounded, Holly thought, as she drank the last of the dark, rich coffee and returned the cup to the saucer. She found him watching her. A shiver of awareness raced through her body. She was letting her emotions get the best of her and that wouldn't do, she thought, placing her napkin on the table.

"Are you ready to leave?" he asked.

As they walked to the parking lot, the smell of the honeysuckle that clung to the high stone-walled fence surrounding the restaurant filled the warm, humid air. The muffled sounds of evening traffic pierced the inky black darkness of the summer night.

"This is my car." She stopped beside a Honda, then searched inside her purse for her keys. She opened the door and stepped behind it, then smiled. "Thanks for dinner."

"You're welcome." He stared at her face. She could see his stern, serious expression clearly under the halogen lamps in the deserted parking lot. His gaze shifted from her eyes to her cheeks, to rest finally on her month.

Her heart beat a little faster with anticipation. He's going to kiss me, she thought. Resisting him was the last thing on her mind. It didn't matter that he was a celebrity and she wanted out of the spotlight. What she wanted more at this very moment was to feel his lips upon hers.

He moved closer to her until the only thing between them was her car door. She could smell the subtle, masculine scent that was uniquely his, mingled with the humid, honeysuckle-perfumed night air.

She shuddered in anticipation at his touch. Mike

tilted her chin and slowly, slowly leaned down until their lips were just a whisper apart. Her lips parted slightly to release tiny gaps of breath.

"Holly," he said softly, his voice dark and sensuous.

"Uhmm?"

"I don't kiss on the first date."

Mike gripped the steering wheel of his Ford Explorer. He'd planned to have dinner with Holly and Wanda to make up for his previous behavior, but as the evening wore on, he couldn't think of anything but Holly Aimes. Holly Aimes and how her dark brown eyes seemed more mystical in the candlelit restaurant. The sweet sound of her laugh and her southern drawl had aroused him all evening long. He maneuvered through the evening traffic to his studio a few miles away.

Tonight, he had no doubt that Holly wanted him just as much as he wanted her, and he *would* have her. He would discover the Holly Aimes that she kept hidden, the Holly that he had seen a brief glimpse of at dinner. She would come to him freely, without reserve or doubt.

Mike stopped at the guard station of the studio and slid his identification in the electronic lock. As the gate opened, he wondered if his assistant had found out anything new about Holly. He wanted to know everything about her, but first he would see if Trey Christian wanted to appear on his show.

* * *

She couldn't concentrate. Holly set aside the financial report and leaned back in her chair. She had been trying to read the report for the past hour, but she'd never gotten past the first paragraph. Since she was a little girl, she'd had been able to focus completely on her assigned task.

The months that she'd spent in hospitals and at home in her bed, recovering from pneumonia, had taught her to finish what she started because she never knew if she would have the energy to finish them the next day or the next hour. As she regained her strength, she learned to block any pain or fear and concentrate on playing with her dolls or reading a storybook.

Today, that skill was beyond her reach; her mind wasn't on business. She was surprised that she'd made it to her office today because she couldn't remember any part of her drive to work. Mike had totally dominated her thoughts. "I don't kiss on the first date," she muttered in disgust. She turned her chair to observe the view of a dense patch of pine trees in the rear of the office buildings.

Last night wasn't a date, no matter how much it felt like one. "I'm glad that we didn't kiss." Her voice broke the silence of the room. If she believed he really meant what he said, she'd have been grateful. She didn't believe it. It was a deliberate action on his part, and she didn't like it at all. Deep inside, she knew that she was lying. She had hungered for his kiss last night. In fact, she had wanted him more than she had ever wanted Trey during their most intimate moments together.

She put aside the memories of the awkward and

sometimes disappointing attempts at lovemaking between her and Trey. The premiere of the movie starring Trey and her brother Robert was three weeks away. When possible, every member of her family went to the premieres of her brother's movies. She would definitely not go to this one, when Trey and her brother Robert would be in the same room. The last time they were together, they'd had a fistfight at the movie studio. Luckily, reporters weren't allowed at the studio. After news of the fight had leaked out, several reporters had showed up on her doorstep, requesting her response. It was almost certain that they would come after her again after the premiere.

All the more reason to study that financial report, she thought, turning back to her desk. According to the balance sheets and cash flow statements, Tamp Security and Alarm Company looked fiscally sound. The preliminary information she had received three months ago contained most of the information contained in this report, but she and Pam had wanted more information before making a decision on purchasing the company.

Of the five companies they'd considered buying, Tamp Security and Alarm was the most financially stable. It had a management style similar to their own. It was the attitude of the owner that had impressed them both. The owner, a sixty-five-year-old former Marine, interviewed them to see if they were the kind of owners who would take care of his employees and customers after he was gone. He wanted to work another year before he retired, and the asking price of the company was fair. The information they'd gathered about Tamp Security and Alarm and the trip to Seattle would be wasted if they didn't win the Milton Group bid.

There was a knock on her door. Holly frowned at the interruption. "Come in," she said.

Pam walked into her office. "Wipe the frown off your face. It's just me." She sat on the edge of Holly's desk. Her orange coat dress stood out against the gray interior of Holly's office. "Did you get a chance to read the report?"

"I just finished," she said. "Everything looks good. All we need is the money."

"You're really serious about moving, aren't you?"

"I'm really serious. Have you heard any more about the bid?"

"No. The Milton Group is keeping things quiet. We'll have to wait until next week to find out who they chose." Pam paused for a moment and studied Holly. "If we don't win this bid, Holly, I want us to get another loan so that we can buy Tamp Security."

"Pam . . ."

Pam held out her hand to interrupt. "I know that you don't want us to get a loan, but it makes sense for us to buy Tamp Security. Their projected profits for next year will make up for the loan payments, and I don't think that we'll get another opportunity to buy a company as good as they are for the price." She paused and smiled sadly at Holly. "As much as I want you to stay here in Atlanta, if you want to move to Seattle and run Tamp Security, I think you should, regardless of what happens with the Milton Group bid."

"I appreciate what you're trying to do." Holly

folded her hands on her desk. "But I can't put us in that kind of financial strain. We both agreed when we started this business that we would not exceed a twenty-percent debt ratio, and buying Tamp Security would put us in the forty-percent range. We can't afford to do that. Thanks for thinking about it."

"Yeah, well . . . I just wanted you to know that I'll support you if you want to move. No matter how abandoned I feel, you just go on and have a great time in Seattle. Don't think about me." She wiped away imaginary tears. "I'll be fine here . . . alone . . . by myself."

Holly laughed at her theatrics. "Speaking of abandon, what happened to Wanda last night?"

"Wanda? I thought she was with you and Mr. Fineness."

"No, she left a message that she couldn't make it. Have you seen her this morning?"

Pam thought for a while, then said no.

Holly picked up her telephone and called Wanda's house. She hung up. "There's no answer."

"Maybe she left a message with Robyn."

Holly called the receptionist and put her on the speakerphone. "Hi, Robyn. Have you heard from Wanda today?"

"Yes, she called early this morning and left a message on the answering machine. Her little sister was sick last night and she's taking her to Egelston Hospital."

"Did she say what was wrong?"

"No, she didn't say."

"Okay. Thanks, Robyn."

Holly pressed a button on the phone to hang up.

"I hope her sister is all right," Pam said with concern.

"Yeah, me too."

"Wait a minute. If Wanda wasn't at dinner with you last night," Pam smiled, "you had dinner with him alone. Details— I want details, *now.*"

"Pam, there *are* no details." She looked down at her desk, not meeting Pam's eyes. "We met at the Private Room when we got the message that Wanda couldn't make it. We decided to eat anyway since we were there. We talked, we ate, we went our separate ways."

"When did you meet at the Private Room, how long did you stay, what did you talk about?" Pam interrogated.

"Have you decided to go to work for the *Atlanta Journal and Constitution?*" Holly sighed. She'd seen that look on Pam's face before. Pam wasn't going to leave until she had answers.

"You better be glad that I waited until today to ask these questions. I started to call you around midnight last night. So what happened?"

"We had dinner and we talked about his chef. That's all."

"That's all? He didn't ask you for a date?"

Holly shook her head no.

"A man doesn't send flowers and a teddy bear without wanting something more than dinner." Pam watched Holly with suspicion.

I'm not telling her, no matter *how* she looks at me, Holly thought. I'm strong. I can handle her pressure tactics. She hoped that her face didn't reveal the discomfort she felt as Pam continued to study her. Pam had learned early on that Holly couldn't lie well.

"You know, you don't look at people when you're trying to hide something." Pam moved off of the desk and stood directly in front of Holly. "I want you to look me directly in the eye and tell me that he didn't ask you for a date." Holly looked into Pam's eyes and began to speak. Pam added, "And he didn't give you any hints that he wanted something other than dinner."

"He didn't ask me for a date and . . ." Her telephone rang. Grateful for the reprieve, Holly reached for the telephone and said, "Hello."

"Wanda, how's your sister?" Holly put her on the speakerphone.

"I don't know," Wanda said, her words filling the office. "The doctor is waiting for some of the test results before he says anything."

"Wanda, this is Pam. You let us know if you need anything, and I mean anything— okay?"

"Okay, I will." There was silence on the line, then Wanda replied. "The doctor wants to talk to me. I'll talk to you later."

The sound of the dial tone filled the office. "She sounded tired," Holly said, after breaking the telephone connection. "If she's still there tonight, I'll go to the hospital and stay with her for a while."

"If you go, call me when you get home." Pam stood and walked out the door.

Holly turned her chair around and faced the window. She hoped that Wanda's little sister wasn't seriously ill. Wanda and her sister were the only survivors in a multicar accident that killed their parents and older brother three years before. Holly remembered the heartache that Wanda had suffered when she'd buried her family and Wanda's strength when she'd given comfort to her grieving sister while dealing with her own.

"Well, worrying won't change a thing," she muttered turning the chair away from the window. She began to work. A few minutes later, Pam stood in the doorway of her office.

"I'll bet you thought that I forgot about those questions that you didn't answer about dinner. I didn't, and I'll get you later." She walked down the hall.

Mike arrived at Holly's office a few hours later. She and Pam were discussing their strategy for another project when Robyn knocked on her office door.

"Mr. Williams is here to see you, Holly."

"Tell him I'm busy," Holly said.

"Send him in," Pam said.

"Hello, Holly." He appeared beside Robyn. "I hope I'm not interrupting anything." His attempt at a serious expression was ruined by the amusement in his eyes.

"Noo-oo," Pam said, using two syllables instead of one, "you're not interrupting anything. We were about to take a break anyway."

Lips pursed, Holly glared at Pam. They weren't about to take a break. In fact, they were in the middle of the project. She turned to him. "Hello, Mike."

He stepped into the room. His multicolored rugby shirt molded the contours of his chest. His jeans looked tailored to his long legs. She never considered the casual look sexy . . . until now.

"Would you like for me to bring in something to drink?" Robyn asked.

"If it's no trouble, Robyn, I'd like a Coca-Cola." He gave her one of his high-voltage, sexy smiles. Robyn stammered something that sounded like "No trouble at all" and closed the door without asking Holly or Pam if they wanted a drink.

She wasn't unaffected by the smile. It brought back memories of the tension between them last night and the kiss that almost was.

"I'll leave you . . ." Pam motioned for the door.

"You don't have to leave," he said. "This won't take long."

"What can I do for you?" Holly asked.

He removed a box that he had hidden behind his back. "I wanted to give you something." He opened the box and put the glass object into her hands.

She studied the glass, then felt heat rush to her face when she recognized the candy inside: chocolate kisses. Holly walked to the table and put the candy jar on her desk. "That wasn't necessary."

"Oh, I think it was *very* necessary." He folded his arms across his chest. "I don't want you ever to say that I haven't given you a kiss."

Pam cleared her throat. "I just thought of a very important phone call I've got to make." She edged her way to the door. "Continue with your conversation."

Before Holly could stop her, Pam walked out of the office and closed the door behind her.

Mike slowly smiled at her. His smile promised heaven, but his eyes hinted at sin. He unfolded his arms and walked to the table and removed a single kiss from the jar. "Want one?" he asked unwrapping the candy. Then he held the tempting chocolate kiss to her lips. The smell of the chocolate was a sweet ambrosia to her senses. He brushed the candy against her mouth, but she kept her lips closed.

She stepped away from him. "No, thanks." Her voice was deeper, huskier than normal.

Without breaking eye contact, he raised the chocolate to his lips, holding it in the exact same spot where it had touched her lips. He lazily bit into it.

Her gaze moved to his mouth, his full, generous mouth. She didn't know when she had begun to hold her breath, but when he slid the other half of the sweet into his mouth, her breath rushed from her lips.

"This is how I imagine you'll taste. Sweet and smooth. The candy is nice, but I want the real thing. When are you going out with me?"

"I . . . I don't think that we should, Mike."

"Then don't think." He gently touched her arms. "Just feel."

She felt so much when he touched her. The thin linen jacket was no obstacle to his warm hands. The heat penetrated through the cloth to her vulnerable skin.

"Say you'll go out with me," he whispered.

"Why are you doing this?"

"Doing what?" He pulled her closer to him. "Asking a beautiful, sexy woman to go out with me?"

She stiffened at the words. The sensual daze that enveloped her disappeared. She stepped out of his embrace. "I'm well aware of how I look. Beautiful isn't the word I would use to describe me."

"You *are* beautiful, Holly."

"The last man who said I was beautiful was my fiancé, and he eloped with a model a week after our engagement."

Holly waited for his reaction. She didn't have to wait long. He closed the distance between them in a heartbeat. "I'm not Trey Christian, and I don't say things that I don't mean, period. You *are* beautiful, Holly. What can I say to make you believe me?" he asked softly, as he cupped her face in his hands. Mike studied her features as if to impart her face to memory. "How can you say you're not beautiful, with eyes that make me want to know all of the secrets they hold?"

Her dark lashes lowered, hiding the spark of pleasure and hint of fear she felt deep within her. *Don't believe him,* her mind warned. *Believe him,* her heart urged.

"Don't play with me," she whispered.

"Look at me."

Her dark brown eyes warily met his determined gaze. "This isn't a game, and I'm not playing. I want you, Holly."

It took her a few seconds to comprehend what he'd said.

"Try that on somebody who doesn't know any better." She moved away from him and sat in her chair, her expression cool and remote.

Mike stood still, watching in frustration as she put as much distance between them as her office would allow. "He really did a number on you, didn't he?"

Neither denying nor acknowledging his statement, she waited for his next move. He was playing the same type of game Trey had played with her, only with Trey, she hadn't known the rules, much less when the game had started.

With a sigh, Mike sat in one of the chairs across from her desk. "I can wait, Holly. Sooner or later, you'll learn that I don't lie."

Holly looked into his warm mahogany eyes. She wanted to believe him, she really did. Somewhere deep inside her heart, she yearned to take a chance. He was nothing like Trey. He didn't mind going to a secluded restaurant, nor did he constantly have people coming and going in his house. Despite his celebrity status, he didn't act like a celebrity when he met her employees. He seemed like a genuinely nice man with some of the same values that she had . . . the kind of man that she wanted to get to know.

Five

Holly cleaned her kitchen cabinets with vigor. The physical work of removing items from the cabinets to the counter and floor, then washing down the empty space was a mindless chore that cleared her mind of weighty problems. The soothing jazz flowed from the den into the kitchen. Neither the music nor the work could keep her thoughts from turning to Mike.

It didn't matter that she had kept the rest of his visit to her office casual. He'd managed to unnerve her with a single stroke of his thumb across her lips. "Why can't he act like an ordinary man?" she muttered, throwing the pine-scented sponge into a bucket of soapy water. He confused her. Mike wasn't the first man to approach her after her bashed engagement. He was the only man who didn't take no for an answer.

She climbed down from the stepladder and emptied the bucket into the sink. The orange-gold rays from the setting sun drifted around the edges of the closed miniblinds on the kitchen windows. Although she hadn't seen reporters around her house lately, she still didn't feel comfortable keeping the curtains and blinds open. "How am I going to handle going out with Mike when I can't even keep the curtains open?" she thought.

The sound of her doorbell interrupted her thoughts. Holly walked to the front door and glanced through the peephole. Her brother stood on the other side. She opened the door and let him in.

"Robert, what are you doing here?" she asked, closing the door when he stepped inside.

"I need to get out of the house. Mama and Daddy are driving me crazy." He gave her a sheepish grin. It was the same grin that he'd used as a little boy when he wanted to get his way. "Can I stay here for a while?"

Holly smiled at him. "Yes, you can stay for a little while." She noticed that he didn't have an overnight bag. "Did you bring extra clothes?"

"No, I'm not spending the night. I'll go back tonight."

She laughed at his pained expression. "I told you to rent an apartment while you were here."

"I know, but I thought that working long hours on the set would give us enough time to visit without getting on each other's nerves."

"They've missed you since you moved to California last year," she said in her parents' defense.

"I missed them, too, but I guess I've been living on my own too long to like living under my parents' roof again."

"I know what you mean. I love them, but I can't imagine the thought of moving back in with them." She shuddered at the thought. "Sometimes the distance between my house and theirs seems too short. I can't wait to move to Seattle."

"You're moving to Seattle?" Robert frowned in confusion.

Holly closed her eyes. *Nice going, Holly.* "I'm planning on moving to Seattle fairly soon."

"Nobody told me you were moving." His frown deepened when he noticed her guilty expression. "You haven't told anyone you're moving, have you?"

"Pam's the only one who knows."

"Why are you moving?"

She was tempted to lie to him, but he knew her too well. "I need to live in a city where I can just be Holly Aimes, not Governor Aimes's daughter, not Trey Christian's ex-fiancée."

"Trey." He said the name as if it were a foul word. "I should have known he'd have something to do with this."

"Listen to me: Trey doesn't matter to me."

"I'll bet you weren't thinking about moving until he ran off and got married."

"You're right. His marriage made me realize that I didn't want my life to be on display for all the world to see."

"I should never have introduced you to him."

"You can't screen the people who come into my life, Robert." She touched his arm. "I'm a grown woman. I make my own mistakes and I make my own decisions."

The chirping ring of the telephone interrupted her.

"Hello."

"Holly, it's Mike."

"How did you get my private number?" she demanded. "I know *I* didn't give it to you."

Robert stared at her, listening without shame to her conversation.

"You didn't?" Mike asked in a playful tone.

"No. I did not."

"Well, I asked Pam for your number."

She gasped in anger.

"But she wouldn't give it to me. So I asked my assistant if he could get your telephone number." When he didn't get a response, he asked, "You don't mind, do you?"

"Yes, I mind," she said sharply.

There was silence on the other end of the phone. "If that's the case," Mike said in a serious tone of voice, "I'll forget that I ever had this number."

"Fine. Why did you call?"

"I called to ask if I could take you and Wanda to dinner after the show tomorrow night. Since Wanda missed dinner the last time, I thought maybe we could go tomorrow night."

"Wanda probably won't be there. Her younger sister is in Egleston Hospital with pneumonia."

"Man, that's too bad. What's her sister's name, and how old is she?"

"Carmen Johnson, and I think she's sixteen. Why?"

"I want to send her a card, maybe some flowers."

"That's really nice." His kind gesture and soft, sexy voice dispelled her anger.

"Don't let the word get out. It'll ruin my image."

"I won't tell anyone that you're a nice guy."

"It's almost time for me to go on the set. Will you go out with me after the show tomorrow?"

She hesitated before answering. She'd had a great time with him when they'd last had dinner together, but was dinner with him worth the risk of dealing with the press? "Yes."

"Then it's a date. Tomorrow after the show."

"I guess so."

" 'Bye, Holly."

" 'Bye, Mike."

Holly put down the phone. She felt a warm contentment inside her. Tomorrow she would be with him again. She would treat him as a casual date. She couldn't afford to get seriously involved with him. The Milton Group should make their decision on the bid soon. Then she wouldn't have time to devote to a serious relationship.

"Who's Mike?" Robert asked, interrupting her thoughts.

"Michael Williams."

"The talk-show host? Are you seeing him?"

"That's none of your business, little brother." Holly looked at the mountain of items that needed to be returned to her cabinets. "If you're going to stay here, you can help me put this stuff back in the cabinets."

"Fine," he said.

She paused at the window as she walked across the room. Hesitantly, she opened the blinds. Golden light filled the room and Holly joined her brother to tackle the countertop covered with items.

Robert glanced at his sister. It wasn't any of his business who she was seeing, he told himself. But this was family. He made a mental note to keep an eye on Mike Williams.

Mike replaced the phone and smiled. Holly had agreed to go out with him without an argument. That was a major accomplishment. She was the most skittish woman he'd ever met— and the most desirable.

He placed the folder with information on Holly in his briefcase. Andy had done an excellent job of getting information on her. Within days, Andy had her private home phone number, address, where she went to church, and a short list of people she considered her friends.

He'd stopped being surprised at the amount of information Andy could supply in a short period of time. What really surprised him was the volume of information that was readily available to the public . . . if you looked deep enough.

Andy had also included a confirmation from Trey Christian's agent to appear on his show next Thursday, the day before the premiere of his next movie. He had a few questions for Mr. Christian, but they would have to wait.

The buzzer from the clock on Mike's desk sounded. He walked out of his office and down the hall to studio E, where his show was taped. There were a thousand details to take care of before the band played the theme song of his show. It was time to get to work.

An hour later, Mike walked onto the stage. The band played the theme song along with the help of trumpeter Herb Alpert. Bright lights illuminated the audience. A rush of adrenaline raced through his body. He could tell from the response of the crowd that this would be one of those nights where everything clicked. As the applause died down, Mike began his monologue.

"Before we begin, I'd like to say hello to a young lady that's in Egleston Hospital, Carmen Johnson. Carmen, you get well, and to your older sister, Wanda, hang in there. It's hard to have a family member in the hospital. And anytime you want tickets to my show, you and your sister can choose any night you want. I'll put in a word with your boss so you can leave work early and get the grand tour." He walked across the stage as another camera made its shot.

"Speaking of bosses. Once a year, the crew around here get to run the show for one day. *One day only!* You heard that, people— one day. They can invite anybody they want on the show, have it in any format, and write the script." A cheer came from one of the cameramen. "This is Brenda." Mike walked over to her. "What was that cheer for? Bring the camera over here."

Holly lay on her bed, watching Mike's show. She should have been in bed hours ago, but instead, she'd watched the late-night news and now Mike's show. She laughed when Brenda, the cameraman, said that she'd invite Denzel, Blair Underwood, Karl Malone, and Mario Van Peebles on the show and all the women in the audience applauded. Not to be outdone, another cameraman said he would invite Julia Roberts and Sharon Stone.

She watched the entire show before she went to sleep. The buzzer from her alarm clock rang early the next morning. After her shower, Holly wandered to her closet and spent some time trying to decide what to wear to work and then to Mike's show. She finally settled for a black raw silk pantsuit. She drank an extra cup of coffee before leaving for work, hoping the caffeine would compensate for her lack of sleep.

The office had a festive atmosphere. Everyone was excited about going to Mike's show tonight. The only grim spot on the day was the news that Wanda's sister hadn't improved during the night.

"Tell me you're not wearing that tonight," Pam asked.

Holly looked down at her clothes. "What's wrong with what I have on?"

"It's too businesslike. You need to wear something that's casual, sexy, subtle."

"I'm fresh out of that this week," Holly said sarcastically. "I just have to settle for black."

"Oh, no, you don't, Holly Michelle Aimes. We're going to buy you some clothes."

"We don't have enough time to go to the store and get clothes."

"I know just the outfit you need," Pam continued, as if Holly had never spoken. "I saw it yesterday at a shop in Little Five Points."

"I'm not going to wear funky clothes."

"Trust me, you'll look good in this."

Pam drove to Little Five Points during the lunch break. Holly tried not to stare at a teenager with an earring and a nose ring connected by a thin chain. The crowd walking on the sidewalk of Euclid Avenue ranged from the jet black hair, painted white face, and black clothing of the death punks to the tie-dye and clogs retro-seventies teenagers.

Pam led her to a small clothing shop. Holly wouldn't have chosen the deep hot pink sleeveless dress, but she had to admit that it looked better than her black pantsuit. With the dress carefully wrapped in plastic and the shoes and earrings they had picked up in another shop, they drove back to the office and worked the rest of the afternoon.

At four o'clock, two minivans with the TTN logo arrived to take them to the studio. When they arrived, they were given the grand tour, starting with the nerve center of the newsroom and ending with the studio where Mike's show was taped. Although Holly was interested in the tour, each time they'd enter a new area, she searched for Mike. She was eager to see him, now that she'd let down her guard. The young college student who'd given them the tour led them to their seats in the first two rows of the studio.

The band started to play upbeat popular tunes while the rest of the audience filed in. The audience consisted of everything from college students in denim cutoffs and short-sleeved cotton shirts to business executives in suits and ties.

Holly smoothed out the skirt of her dress and waited anxiously for the show to begin. When the band played the theme song, she sat up straight in her seat. The noise from the audience nearly drowned out the band. She clapped when Mike confidently walked out on stage wearing his signature suit and tie. He looked at home in the business suit, serious yet playful. Later that night, she wouldn't be able to recall who the guests were on his show. It was Mike who had held her attention.

When the show was over, she was led backstage by the same guide while Pam and the rest of the employees went back to the vans. She received a few curious looks, but the crew seemed to be friendly.

Mike stood talking to two members of the studio crew. He motioned Holly over to the group.

"Hi," she said softly.

"Hi. I'd like you to meet Diane Selle, my producer, and you've already met Andy Kurtz." The two said hello. "I'm going to be here for a while. Why don't you wait in my office for me? I promise not to keep you waiting too long."

"All right. Nice to meet you both."

Mike's office was huge. A large-screen television, a VCR, and an impressive stereo system occupied a small space along one wall. Bookshelves lined the rest of the walls. His desk sat in the middle of the room. A sofa and loveseat were grouped around the television.

"Would you like anything to drink, Ms. Aimes?" the guide said.

"No, thanks," Holly said, as she walked over to the sofa.

"If you want to watch TV or a video, use this remote." He gave her the remote control. "The tape library is here, and the same remote controls the stereo and the cassette tapes. CDs are over here."

Holly watched in amazement as the young man

opened the drawers that contained row after row of videos and CDs. When she assured him that she would be fine alone in the office, she picked a video-tape, placed it in the VCR, and relaxed on the sofa. Halfway through the movie, Mike entered his office.

Holly put the tape on pause. "I can't believe you have *Harlem on the Prairie*. My father talks about this movie all the time."

"I think I have all of the black cowboy movies that were ever made. My grandfather told me about those movies when I was little. I didn't think I'd ever find copies of them. Do you want to watch the rest of the tape?"

"Yes, if you don't mind."

"I don't mind at all. I'll call the guards at the main gate and let them know that we're still here." Mike walked to his desk and picked up the tele-phone. A few minutes later, he sat next to her on the sofa and put his arm around her shoulders.

"What happened to the rest of the people?"

Mike looked at his watch. "Most of them should be on their way home by now. For the most part, we're the only ones here."

Holly found it hard to concentrate on the movie. They were all alone. His warm hand absently ca-ressed her bare shoulder and the heat of his body engulfed her.

As the cowboys raced across the desert in search of the bad guys, Holly's own heart raced. Just sitting next to him was a turn-on. He didn't wear cologne, but the rough, masculine scent of him aroused her.

When the final credits rolled on the screen,

Holly turned to him and was trapped in the sensual web of his gaze.

"This is our second date." He slowly lowered his lips to hers. "I *do* kiss on the second date." His lips touched hers. Fire. Ice. The kiss ignited a flame within her that burned red-hot and froze her simultaneously. His hands gently touched her cheeks in long, lingering strokes. All too quickly, he raised his head, breaking the physical bond between them. Reluctantly, Holly opened her eyes.

Mike removed the remote control from her hand and turned off the television. "We'd better go if we're going to have dinner."

How could he just stop like that, she thought, as she stood, her legs trembling. The kiss obviously didn't affect him as much as it had affected her. When they reached the door to his office, he grasped her shoulders and turned her toward him. She didn't have time to prepare for the onslaught to her senses. All the emotions that were missing in the first kiss, he poured into this kiss. It wasn't a gentle kiss.

He nudged her lips apart and with his tongue stroked her from within, passionately, completely. When he'd tasted his fill, he spread kisses on her cheeks, her jaw, her neck. She had never felt so overwhelmed and so wanted. His hands rubbed her shoulders, sometimes massaging, sometimes holding her in a fierce embrace. Gradually, the kisses became less urgent until he barely touched her lips to his.

He leaned his head against hers and held her

tenderly. His breath was harsh, as if he'd been running. Her chest rose and fell roughly.

Raising his head, he looked into her eyes. She could see the lingering desire. Silently, he stepped away from her and opened the door to his office.

"Let's go." His voice was husky and rough.

They walked through the dimly lit studio. Her legs felt shaky and weak. How could she deal with a man who made her feel this weak? The kisses she'd shared with Trey were nothing like the kiss she and Mike had just shared. She'd always felt that she was missing something when she was with Trey. Now she knew that passion was what was lacking in that relationship. Her heart was still racing when they reached his car.

Mike helped her inside and walked around to the driver's side. He turned to her and asked, "What do you have a taste for?"

Holly looked at her watch. It was midnight. "It doesn't matter, so long as the restaurant is quiet and not too crowded."

Mike drove to Dailey's, a small restaurant on the north side of town. Dailey's attracted the yuppie crowd. Pristine white linens, ornate silverware, and fragile china dressed discreetly distant tables. They were led to a secluded table in the corner of the restaurant.

"Are you going to hide behind the menu all night?" Mike asked.

"No, I was just trying to decide what to order." She placed the menu on the table, then folded her hands in her lap.

"Good, I . . ." He paused when the waiter came

to the table. They quickly ordered their food. "So what did you think of the show?"

"I thought it was fun. Everybody must work really hard to get the show ready each night."

"It *is* hard, but the people I work with are a good group. They make my job easier. It's the guests that sometimes make our job a living hell. Some don't show up and won't call in advance to tell us. Others want to tell us how to run the show. It can be a mess sometimes."

"No kidding. I would have thought that they came to the studio, did the interview, and left."

"Don't I wish," Mike laughed. "Some guests are like that; others want to be catered to, and if an interview doesn't go well, I usually hear about it after the show."

"There's nothing like an irate customer, is there? No matter what you do to try to make them happy, it's still your fault."

Mike hesitated, then smiled reluctantly. "I at least apologized when I made a mistake. Let's not get ugly, now."

"I would never get ugly. Well, maybe just a little."

"Just be glad that millions of people aren't watching when *you* make a mistake. You wouldn't believe the mail and phone calls that come into my office."

"But you get fan mail, too. Don't try to make me believe that your job is so bad. I read somewhere that women send you all kinds of, er, intimate apparel."

"I got one pair of panties in the mail and a few weeks later the papers made it seem like I get panties in the mail everyday. You should know not to believe everything that you read in the newspaper or hear on TV. If you want to know something about me, ask me." There was an angry edge to his voice.

Holly was slightly taken aback. "Okay, I will. Why do you let your people run the show once a year?"

"Contrary to popular belief, I don't know everything."

"No!" She responded with mock horror.

"Yes. It's true. When I let people try things their way, they generate a lot of new, innovative ideas. They also get some junk, but that's to be expected."

"Aren't you afraid that they'll do something to hurt the show or your career?"

"No. To most of the people, this is their chance to show their stuff." He leaned closer to Holly, causing her heart to skip a beat. "If an idea works well and I use it on future shows, I reward them. If someone shows talent in another position, I let them try it out for a time, and if they're good, I move them to that position. For me and my people, it's a win-win situation." Mike paused. "Now, I want to ask you a question." His expression was somber. "Are you still in love with Trey Christian?"

She took her time in answering. She knew the answer, but what she didn't know was his reason for asking the question. Did she trust him enough to share that part of her history with him? Would he use what she said, as material for his show? Holly studied him beneath lowered lashes. Yes, she did trust him. He hadn't taken advantage of the situation in his office tonight when she was vulnerable. "No, I'm not still in love with Trey."

"That's good. Then there's no reason *we* can't have a relationship."

"Yes, there is. In fact, there are two. One, I'm going to be moving to Seattle next year, and two, I don't want to be in the public eye anymore. I've been in the spotlight most of my life, and I want to be able to leave my house or office without a reporter waiting to take my picture."

"You're moving because of what happened with Trey Christian? You were going to marry a movie actor whose career depends on his being in the spotlight. Don't let him make you leave your home!"

Holly gave a heavy sigh. "It's not just Trey; Trey was the last straw. It's the press in general. I seem to be good target practice for reporters. My personal life isn't personal anymore, and I've had to literally hide from reporters just to be left alone."

"How did you handle the press before? Why didn't you move away years ago?"

Before she could answer, the waiter returned with their meal. When the food was placed before them and the waiter had left, she answered his questions.

"I *tried* to ignore the press. My family doesn't have a problem with the attention. I thought that I could be like them and just brush off the bad things that were written about me, which wasn't much. The worst thing that happened to me before Trey was that I was called the ugly duckling in the family of swans. After Trey got married, I couldn't go anywhere without someone taking a picture. My friends were also asked to do interviews about us. I can't deal with the fishbowl existence I've been forced to live with."

"Why did you agree to go out with me? I'm not a recluse and I'm in the spotlight."

"It's simple." Her posture took on a professional demeanor. "In a few months, I'll be in Seattle and you'll still be here in Atlanta. Any time that we spend together will be temporary. If the press should see us together, I can always use our business relationship as a cover. To the outside world, we're business associates."

"What about when we're alone?" he said.

"Given the amount of time that we'll have together, I don't think we can be more than friends."

"What if we become more than friends, Holly? What then?"

She froze, then slowly released the tension in her shoulders. *Get a grip, Holly. That will never happen.* "Hypothetically speaking, if by some chance we become more than friends, I'll expect that we'll be discreet. Very discreet. I wouldn't want the press to know about it."

Mike carefully placed his fork on his plate and subjected Holly to the full force of his gaze before he spoke. "Don't kid yourself, Holly. We will be more than friends. Whether you're here or in Seattle won't matter at all."

"I think I have some say in that, and I believe you're wrong . . . dead wrong."

"If you believe that, then you have nothing to worry about." Mike raised his glass in a toast. "To friendship."

"To friendship." Holly took a sip of wine. Did

he think he could just tell her what to do? He was in for a big surprise if he did. She'd been a pushover once; she'd never be one again. Besides, when would they see each other? They both had very demanding, time-consuming careers. The move to Seattle would take up most of her time, but deep in her heart, she knew that the danger of caring for him was there, hovering between them like dark, rolling clouds just before a thunderstorm. The passion she felt for him couldn't be denied, no matter how much she wanted it to go away.

"What do you plan to do in Seattle?"

Holly told him about her plans to open a second branch of Security Force and how much of the plan depended on winning the Milton Group bid.

"Holly?"

Holly turned at the sound of her name. Walking toward their table were her father, her stepmother, her half-sister, and her date. They stopped at the table. They were four beautiful people. Holly looked down at her dress. The pink dress that she wore suddenly didn't look as pretty as it had earlier.

Her stepmother, Jean, wore a formal summer dress of pale peach that looked wonderful with her golden brown skin. Her half-sister, Sandra, wore a white dress. She saw Mike look at both women and felt like a frump.

"This is a nice surprise," her father said. Mike stood to shake his hand.

"We just left the Alliance Theater," her stepmother joined in. "I just had to come here for dessert. Dailey's makes the best chocolate cheesecake." Jean rambled on in a slow, syrupy tone that she could change at the drop of a hat to a rapid northern accent.

"We came over from Mike's show over here." When she saw the speculative look pass between Jean and her father, Holly quickly added that the whole staff of Security Force had gone to the show.

"You won't mind if we join you, do you?" Jean asked. She was already motioning for the waiter.

"Mother, they might not want a crowd at their table," Sandra said, trying to stop her mother. Holly flashed her a grateful look, but she knew it was too late. Jean's heart-shaped face and curly sandy-brown hair gave her the appearance of a delicate southern belle, but a steel-like will lay below the surface. Her clear amber eyes gleamed with determination.

The waiters quickly added another table and four chairs. When the others were finally settled, Jean began doing what she did best: pulling personal information from people. Jean had met her match with Mike. Within five minutes, he had diverted Jean's questions about himself and was asking her his own questions.

Holly lowered her head and smiled. When she looked up from her plate, she caught her father's wink. But the evening was dimmed by her feelings of inadequacy. The joy and excitement were gone from the evening. With Jean on her right and Sandra, a younger version of her mother, on her left, she felt as attractive as a plate of chopped liver. As the evening progressed, she became quiet, letting the conversation flow around her instead of participating. Mike seemed to be having a good time, she thought. He kept his side of the conversation flowing. He joked with her father and Sandra's boyfriend and charmed Jean and Sandra. For the first time tonight, Holly wished that the evening would end.

Mike watched as Holly became more withdrawn. His attempts to draw her into the conversation were met with monosyllabic answers. The opened, relaxed woman became quiet and aloof. She sat with her shoulders slumped forward, head held down. She looked as if she was trying to make herself invisible. He looked at the group to see if the others had noticed her body language. They seemed oblivious to her discomfort.

He studied both sisters. They were very different from each other. Sandra, undeniably pretty with a high-yellow complexion, heart-shaped face, and light brown eyes, and Holly, appealing and sexy, with medium brown complexion and dark brown eyes. Although Holly didn't resemble her father either, with his honey brown skin and dark brown eyes, she stood out like a hawk among canaries. But unlike that bird of prey, she held herself in low esteem.

When his eyes met Holly's, he saw a flash of emotion that he didn't recognize. Puzzled, he continued to watch her, but she didn't meet his gaze again. After that incident, she seemed to grow more withdrawn. What was wrong with her? Did she not get along with her sister?

Mike waited until he felt they could leave without offending the rest of the group.

"Would you excuse us? Holly and I have to

leave." Mike motioned for the waiter. "It was nice to see you again. Let me take care of the dessert."

"That's not necessary," Holly's father argued.

"Not necessary, but it's something that I want to do."

"Will we see you again?" Jean asked.

He knew what she was asking. Mike looked at Holly before replying, "You'll be seeing me around." Holly frowned at his response. Well, she'll get used to having me around, he thought, as he watched her hug her sister and stepmother, then kiss her father goodbye.

They made their way to the entrance of the restaurant. Holly stood to the side, waiting for Mike to settle the bill. As they walked to the parking lot, he wondered if he could recapture the feelings that they'd had before her family had come.

"Holly, what's wrong?"

How could she tell him what she felt, she thought, without sounding petty? How could she tell him that she saw his expression when he looked from her to Sandra? She knew that he wondered how two people in the same family looked so different. The comparison between them was inevitable, and she didn't blame him for looking at Sandra. Sandra was beautiful, and she was only adequate.

How could she explain her feeling of alienation when she was with her family? She was a member of the family, but looked nothing like the other members. She would have thought she was adopted, except that she was the image of her mother.

She had no explanation for her feelings. "Nothing's wrong."

"Holly, you changed when your family joined us. Do you not get along with them?"

"Of course I get along with them," she said hotly, as she walked to the passenger side of his car, waiting for him to unlock the door.

He opened the door and helped her inside. When he climbed into the driver's side, he paused for a moment and looked at her. Holly breathed a sign of relief when he started the car. For an instant, he looked like he was going to continue to question her. He drove through the streets of Atlanta, heading to Decatur. They didn't speak until he drove to her office, where she'd left her car.

"I'll follow you home," he said.

"You don't have to do that."

"I'm going to follow you home." He unlocked the door and walked her to her car. He was her own private escort to her home. When she reached her house, he parked his car in the driveway and walked her to the door.

"Thanks for the show and dinner," she said.

Mike put his hand on the doorframe, trapping her between the door and his body. For a long time, he stared into her eyes as if he was searching for something. Slowly he lowered his lips to hers. He gave her time to reject the kiss before pressing his lips to hers in a brief, sweet kiss.

"Goodnight, Holly."

Six

Holly watched the sun rise Saturday morning from the large window in her bedroom— not because she wanted to, but because she had spent most of the night tossing and turning in her bed. Unanswered questions kept her awake most of the night. Was she doing the right thing in seeing Mike? Or was she setting herself up for a fall?

She had been so sure of herself before her family had showed up at the restaurant. She was like a distant star, and her family was the bright midday sun. The star was a pale reflection of the real thing. As a child, she had been ignored time and time again when a member of her family had entered the room.

Holly had tried hard to be like her flamboyant family. She'd taken dance lessons and music classes and even entered a local beauty pageant in an attempt to be outgoing— and failed miserably. With each failure, Holly felt that she'd let her family down. Sometimes, she would go to her room and cry, longing for the days when her mother was alive and she belonged. Over the years, she'd become accustomed to staying in the background while her family sparkled in the limelight. She was a part of the family, yet different.

Somehow, the thought of letting down her family again was too much for her last night. Although her family never blamed her for the break-up with Trey, Holly felt that she had failed them. They had tried to shield her from reporters during the weeks after her broken engagement and stood beside her when she finally ventured into public again, but she always felt that she hadn't lived up to their expectations.

Holly turned from the window and walked to the bathroom to take a shower.

There was a knock at her back door. She put down her book, wondering who it could be. She could see Mike's face through the glass.

"What are you doing at the back door?" she asked.

"I didn't think you'd want me to go to the front door with a reporter from the *Atlanta Journal* camped out across the street."

"Oh, no." She ran to the window in her living room. Peering through the white sheers, she saw a car parked across the street. The driver's-side window was rolled down to relieve the midmorning summer heat. Inside the car, a man with a camera watched her house.

"How did you get past him?" she asked, turning from the window.

"I parked my car on the street behind you and went through your neighbors' backyard."

Holly shook her head and smiled at his ingenuity. "So, do you want to go out?"

"I'm not going outside with that reporter setting in the front yard."

"He'll never know that you're gone. Just follow me."

And follow him she did. She locked her back door. Her backyard was filled with tall pine trees with neatly landscaped pine islands grouping them together. She never considered her backyard as an escape route, but that was exactly what it would be today. Mike carefully walked along the back of the house until he reached a large holly bush. He motioned for Holly to stay at the door, then he looked around the bush and walked back to Holly.

"The coast is clear. Let's go." Mike grasped her hand and they raced across her backyard, dodging pine trees and the slippery pine straw. Mike helped her climb the chain-link fence and jump down on the other side.

They were midway through the neighbors' backyard when the back door opened and her neighbor, Mr. Walker, walked out. Mr. Walker paused, then glared at the two. He thought that he'd stopped the neighborhood kids from cutting through his backyard. "What are you kids doing in my yard?" His voice was strong and loud. It didn't sound like the voice of a sixty-two-year-old retiree.

Holly and Mike looked at each other. Holly felt like she'd been caught by the principal. She hoped that Mike could think of something, because right now she couldn't think of a single explanation.

Mike took control of the situation. "Sir, I'm Mike Williams, and we need your help."

Mr. Walker gave him a suspicious look.

"What kind of help?"

"There's a reporter parked in the yard of that house." Mike pointed to Holly's house. "We're trying to get away from him and get to my car, so we need to go through your yard."

He squinted his eyes and studied the two. They were older than he'd first thought, and if he'd been wearing his glasses, like his wife had told him to, he would have realized it. At least his wife didn't have to know about this. "You're not in trouble, are ya?"

"No, sir. We just want to have a little peace and quiet."

He sighed. "Go ahead, but don't make this a habit. I don't want a footpath through my yard." Mr. Walker watched them walk across his yard, shaking his head, walked over to his toolshed, and began to tend to his perfectly manicured lawn.

Holly felt like a teenager sneaking out of the house at night. Her glance swept the neighborhood; she hoped that they wouldn't be discovered. The fear of discovery was outweighed by the thrill of the escape. She was startled when he grasped her hand. Looking at his face, she saw the strength behind his mischievous expression. She smiled. The tension and fear that she felt earlier seemed to go away. Holding his hand, she walked with him to his car, which was parked two houses down.

"Where are we going?" Holly asked, as she fastened her seat belt.

"Why don't you show me Atlanta?"

"All right, I'll show you a different Atlanta." She directed him down I-20 to the West End. She showed him the Atlanta that was rich with history of African-Americans. Sweet Auburn Avenue had once been the home of several successful businesses. The area was now aged and a faded imitation of what it had once been. Mike parked the car and they walked down the street.

"That was the Top Hat Club. My grandmother said she and granddaddy would come here for a show. The entertainers would have played at a white club the night before." They walked past the vacant brick building. The windows and doors had been boarded up long ago. A few cars drove down the street. The sidewalk was cracked in places. Holly studied Mike's face. He looked up at the buildings and turned to her.

"Why did you pick this place?" He pointed at another empty building. "This doesn't look like Atlanta. It looks dead."

"It's not dead. Every year there's a Sweet Auburn Festival. Merchants from all over the world come to the festival and entertainers perform concerts before huge crowds. But it's the history that makes it come alive."

He still looked puzzled.

"Come on, let's go to the APEX museum and you'll see what I mean." Holly walked down the street to the side entrance of the museum. The museum was empty. They were the only people there besides the curator and an aide. The display was of African-American photographers and their work.

Photographs from the 1800s to the 1950s were displayed. They stopped in front of a picture of a black family standing in front of a Victorian house. The description said "Auburn Avenue, 1904."

"This is the same street. Look at this." She pointed to a group of pictures. One was of a street filled with people going to different businesses. Another was the interior of a plush barbershop with ornate chandeliers and comfortable chairs.

"It looks like a nice place," Mike said.

"That's Alonzo Herdon's shop. He founded Atlanta Life Insurance and was a very wealthy man. As matter of fact, his house isn't too far from here, if you want to see how wealthy black Atlantans lived during the early 1900s." She turned away from the photographs to look at him.

He was standing right beside her. His warm, masculine scent surrounded her senses, making her very aware of him. His gaze locked with hers. She forgot what she was about to say. The old photographs seemed to fade around her. Her focus was on Mike. The friendly camaraderie between them was overshadowed by the blatantly sexual look in his eyes.

"Holly," he said, in a deep, raspy voice.

She shivered at the sound of her name. So much of his need for her was conveyed in his saying her name, a need that was echoed deep with her being and called to the very heart of her.

His strong, rough fingers caressed her cheek. The warmth of his touch spread throughout her body. Her lips parted as she tried to fill her lungs with air. The simple act of breathing became secondary to the desire to taste his lips once again.

He lowered his head toward hers. She closed her eyes and felt the magic touch of his lips to hers.

Slowly, lovingly, gently, he mated his lips to hers. She knew that this was what she'd been waiting for all morning long: his feel, his taste, his touch. His thumb caressed her cheek in slow movements. Then his other hand moved to her waist, drawing her against his warm, strong body.

Ever so slowly, he urged her into a web of desire that enticed her totally . . . completely.

A piercing beep sounded as the door of the museum opened and a group of people entered. Holly released his shoulders. She didn't remember hugging him. She turned and stepped away from him and stared blindly at the photographs on the wall.

What was going on, she wondered. She'd never kissed anyone in public before. Public displays of affection always made her uncomfortable, but she hadn't thought of anything but Mike when he'd kissed her. Not even Trey had ever made her forget about the possibilities of reporters being around ready to take her picture, but Mike had made her do just that with a kiss.

She could hear the harsh sound of Mike trying to catch his breath. Then she felt his hands on her shoulders. His hands trembled as they rested there. She stood there quietly, trying to regain her composure.

"Let's get out of here," Mike said. He guided her to the door, paused, removed money from his wallet, and dropped it into the donation box.

The bright, hot afternoon sun made the walk back to his car uncomfortable. They rolled down the windows when he drove out of the parking lot. Holly directed him out of the city of Atlanta. They stopped at an ice-cream parlor and drove to a small neighborhood park. Underneath a canopy of leaves, they ate their ice cream and watched a group of children play no-holds-barred soccer.

"Those two look like me and my oldest brother, Stephen." Mike pointed to two boys fighting over the soccer ball.

"You and your brother used to fight?"

"Yeah," he smiled. "We would fight about anything. If he said it was black, I'd say it was white, and if he had something, then I wanted it." He scooped out a spoonful of his ice cream and ate it. Holly watched the spoon disappear between his lips, remembering the taste of him on her lips after they'd kissed. She pulled her gaze away from his lips and began eating her own ice cream.

"He was the one who would beat up anybody that picked on me in the neighborhood. It didn't matter that he picked on me, but nobody else could do it if he was around."

"You sound like the two of you were close."

"The three of us are. I've got a younger brother named David. The three of us were constantly getting on each other's nerves." He turned to her. "You know how it is. I'm sure you and your brother and sister argued."

"Not really. I'm six years older than my brother and eight years older than my sister. I didn't argue with them very much, but I did break up most of their fights."

Mike listened intently to her. What she didn't say said more about her family life than what she did confess. The gap in age wasn't the only gap between Holly and her siblings.

"Don't tell me that they didn't do something to embarrass you in front of your friends, like take something out of your room?"

"No. By the time they could do something like that, dad was running for mayor and we were all supposed to project the right image to the public. No fussing. No fighting. No crying," she said with a laugh.

He could hear the loneliness in her voice, no matter how much she tried to hide it. He could almost see her as a little girl, feeling like she wasn't really a part of the family and told to act a certain way in front of hundreds, maybe thousands, of people.

"What was it like when your father ran for office? How old were you then?"

When she didn't answer, he followed her gaze to the children playing soccer. He thought that she was going to ignore his question, but then in a low voice she began to speak.

"I was thirteen when Daddy ran for a seat on the city council. I remember him being gone all the time, and when he was home he was tired. Then, one day, he took us out campaigning with him. There were reporters there, because it was a tight race. We were all standing together and I remember one of his volunteers asking another if I was

adopted, because I didn't look like the others."
Holly paused.

Mike longed to smooth the frown on her face.
Her eyes were clouded with the pain she'd experienced so long ago.

She cleared her throat as if to dispel those old
feelings and began to speak. "That was the first
time that I felt completely alienated from my family,
like I didn't belong. I wanted to yell at that lady
that I was there from the very beginning. During
that campaign, I was referred to as the child from
his first marriage. I really hoped that daddy would
lose so that I wouldn't have to go through that
again." She looked at him, gauging his reaction.
"At thirteen, I was pretty self-absorbed. But Daddy
won and I learned to deal with being considered
an outsider by people other than my family."

"Didn't you tell your father how you felt?"

"When? I rarely saw him at home, and I didn't
think that he could do anything about it." She
waved her hand as if to brush off the question.

"Hmm," he said, letting the conversation end.
He watched her eat another spoonful of her ice
cream, wondering how any parent could be oblivious to the kind of hurt that Holly had experienced.

He was angry with her parents for letting her go
through that pain alone and for letting her get hurt
in the first place. He felt a fierce wave of protec-
tiveness toward her and he wanted to hold her in
his arms and erase the hurt and pain that she'd
experienced. He put the top on his empty ice cream
container and put it aside. He'd never felt protective

of the women he'd dated before, but then again, he'd never dated someone like Holly.

Holly was the type of woman who made a man think of marriage and children. The two things that he had delegated to later in his life now seemed appealing. Under the cool shade, they watched the children run back and forth, chasing the soccer ball. She placed her empty ice cream carton next to his. He studied her face. Twin lines formed between her brow as she looked at the children. He reached out and brushed his fingers across her brow. She turned to him in surprise. The frown disappeared and she smiled at him. That was more like it. He leaned back against the trunk of the tree and pulled her with him until her shoulders rested on his chest. He wrapped his arms around her. The sweet smell of freshly cut grass mingled with the light, floral scent of her perfume.

"All I need is a hammock and I could stay here forever," he said lazily.

"The gnats and mosquitoes would pick you up and carry you off."

"This is my daydream." He nudged her shoulders. "There are no bugs in my daydream."

"I suppose that the temperature doesn't get above eighty and there are no police to arrest you for vagrancy, either."

"Work with me on this one, Holly, work with me," he laughed. "Now, where was I?"

"You were in a hammock."

"Yeah. There aren't any bugs, and the weather's perfect. I've got an Emmy for best director of a television movie."

Holly tilted her head back and looked at him. "You want to direct television movies? What about your show?"

"I won't always be a talk-show host." His eyes met hers. "I want to try my hand at directing. I like made-for-television movies and I plan to direct one as soon as I find the right script." She settled against his chest once more and he continued. "Back to my daydream. I've got an Emmy and I'm taking a rest before the next picture. There's just you and me lazing away the day in the hammock."

He felt her tense in his arms. He knew he had step across the line with his reference to the two of them as a couple, but if he left it up to Holly to decide when their relationship would move forward, he would be waiting a long time. He sighed, then held her hand. "But that's just my dream." The tension in her shoulders faded away. He let her off the hook for now, but soon she would have to face the fact that they were going to be lovers and not just friends.

"What about you? What would be your perfect daydream?"

"Oh, I don't know."

"Come on. You've got to have a dream."

She thought for a moment. "My perfect day would be in the spring, just before the mosquitoes became really awful. Flowers would be in full bloom. I'd be able to go anywhere I wanted and nobody would pay attention to me. I'd be just another woman walking down the street." She looked at him. "That would be my dream."

Mike was torn. He wanted her to fulfill her

dream, but in doing so, he would have to be out of her life completely. He didn't want to think about that possibility. He had to persuade her to change her dream to include him. He didn't know why it was so important that he be a part of her life, but it was.

They sat in silence, each wrapped in his own thoughts. The sound of a shriek of laughter broke the introspective mood. They laughed as they watched a toddler try to catch a large rubber ball. Each time the child would get close to the ball, he would kick it away. Finally, he caught the ball and carried it back to his mother.

A few minutes later, they decided to walk off the ice cream. They shared the sidewalk with skaters wearing helmets and knee pads. Slowly, they made their way around the park, stopping once so that Mike could push Holly in a swing.

A woman walking her dog did a double-take when she saw Mike, but she kept walking. Mike didn't react, but Holly felt a jolt of fear when the woman looked at them. The relaxed feeling that she had while they were walking was gone. She walked faster, as if she was trying to hide.

"Slow down, Holly. This isn't a race," Mike said, pulling her back to his side.

"That woman recognized you."

"So?"

"So! People will want your autograph, and then a crowd will form . . ."

"Holly, look around. Nobody's paying attention to us."

She looked. He was right. People were going

about their business and enjoying the park. She looked at him sheepishly. "Sorry, I'm just paranoid. When Trey and I went out, people would always crowd around us."

I'll bet Trey deliberately brought attention to himself, Mike thought, but he kept his opinion to himself. He reached for her hand and said, "Pretend the other people aren't here and enjoy the park."

They continued to walk, their hands joined. Holly enjoyed the rest of the time they spent in the park. It was almost like her perfect daydream. No one watched her as she walked by. The other people on the sidewalk didn't recognize either of them. They decided to leave when they reached the parking lot.

Holly directed him through the old homes surrounding the Emory University campus. The brick Tudor-style houses were surrounded by large, well-manicured yards. Old money had kept the neighborhood intact.

They meandered their way to Holly's neighborhood. Mike drove down her street. The reporter was still parked in front of her house. Mike drove around the block and parked his car in front of Mr. Walker's house.

"We'd better ask if we can go through his yard," she said.

"Sometimes it's better to ask for forgiveness than to ask permission." With that, he opened the door and walked around to open the door for her.

"Remember, I have to deal with him when you're not here. I think we should ask permission."

"What are you going to do if he says no?"

"Walk through another yard." She walked to the front door of the Walker home. Mr. Walker opened the door.

"Are you back again?" He tilted his head back to see his neighbor clearly with his trifocals.

"Uh. Yes, sir," Holly said. "I wanted to know if we could go through your yard one last time?"

"Well, I guess it won't hurt."

"Thank you," she said, and hurried across the front yard.

"I still think we should have just walked back there," Mike said. He helped her over the fence before climbing over it himself. They walked across her back yard. The afternoon sun shone brightly through the tall pine trees. She opened the back door and invited him inside.

"Would you like something cold to drink?" she asked, leading him into the den. She didn't want the afternoon to end, but now that they were alone in her home, she was nervous. "I've got sweet tea, Coke, and juice." She stood in the doorway between the kitchen and the den, hoping she didn't look as nervous as she felt.

"Anything would be fine with me, as long as it's cold."

She left him wandering around the den when she went into the kitchen. She removed two glasses from the cabinet. Her hands shook when she put ice in the glass, then poured the iced tea. She put the pitcher of tea back into the refrigerator. "Get a grip," she told herself, then took a deep, calming breath before joining Mike.

He stood before her large collection of books.

The sunlight from the windows spread rays of light on the bookshelves and across his broad shoulders. His stone-washed jeans did nothing to hide his firm buttocks and long, muscular legs.

She must have made a noise, because he turned to her. For a moment she stood mesmerized by his gaze. She felt desire, strong and deep. Her hands tightened around the cold glasses.

"Here's your tea." She walked toward him with a glass outstretched in front of her. Their fingers touched as he took the glass. Taking a sip of the cool, sweet liquid, she struggled to think of something to say. She stared into the icy brown tea. The hum of the air conditioner filled the silence in the room. The silence stretched and stretched. Finally, she worked up enough nerve to look at him. He stood there smiling at her.

"I thought you were going to stare into that glass for the rest of the day."

She laughed, "No."

"I'm not going to change into Mr. Hyde just because we're alone." He waved his glass at the books. "You've got quite a collection. Have you read them all?"

"Most of them," she answered, with a hint of pride in her voice.

He picked up an oversized book. "Grimm Brothers' Fairy Tales?"

"What can I say, I like fairy tales."

He placed the book back on the shelf and walked around the coffee table to the sofa. Patting the cushion next to him, he motioned for Holly to sit.

"Come on, I won't bite . . . unless you want me to." His expression was comically lecherous.

She looked at him, unsure if he was joking or not. When he wiggled his eyebrows, she laughed and sat next to him. "Are you always like this?"

"Like what?"

"I don't know." Holly looked at the ceiling for inspiration. "Unpredictable."

"I'm not unpredictable. I always know what I'm doing."

"That's what I mean. You don't do what I expect you to do."

"What *did* you expect me to do?"

"Respond with a serious answer, maybe."

"You want serious . . . how's this?" He straightened his shoulders. All trace of laughter was gone from his eyes. He frowned as if in deep concentration. "You take life entirely too seriously, Holly. I think you need to lighten up." His brown eyes were clear and bright with honesty and sincerity.

"Have you been talking to Pam? She's always telling me to lighten up."

"Great minds think alike."

"Or demented minds."

He smiled at her. Slowly the smile melted away. She didn't recognize the emotion behind his expression, but it called to her, stripping away her defenses.

"I like you, Holly Aimes."

"I like you, too, Mike," she said, with a bit of surprise. She really did like him.

"Don't sound so surprised."

"Oh, no. I didn't mean it to come out that way."

"But you are surprised that you like me. Admit it." He pushed her shoulder. "Admit it."

"Okay," she laughed. "I'm surprised that I like you. I didn't expect to, especially after talking to you over the phone about your alarm system."

"You condemn me on the bases of one telephone call." He shook his head.

"Our first meeting wasn't that great, either."

"Would you be friendly if the police were giving you yet another fine?"

"No, but you didn't have to be so nasty, and it was your fault the alarm didn't work."

"I apologized for that. You didn't want to let me make up for it anyway. I admit it when I make one of my very rare mistakes."

"That what I really like about you, Mike. You're so modest."

"Hang around with me and you'll learn that I'm smart and handsome, too."

Holly tried to keep a straight face but failed. Soon they were both laughing. She would remember their laughter later that evening when he'd left and she wondered if she was smart to let herself enjoy the time with him when she would be leaving so soon.

Seven

Sunday had become Holly's lazy day. Until a few months ago, she would have driven to the Mount Carmel Baptist Church. She had attended early morning services there since she was a little girl. But that had come to an end when a reporter had sat beside her in church and begun asking questions about Trey's marriage.

So today, she rose early and prepared a light breakfast and leisurely ate it while reading the paper. She had planned to visit Wanda's sister yesterday, until Mike had come over and she had forgotten about her plans until late that night.

Holly took a shower, then dressed in her favorite jeans, teal-green cotton shirt, and canvas shoes. She went to the living room window and peered through the curtains. To her relief, the street was free of cars. Grabbing her purse, she walked to her garage and started her car.

Traffic was light as she drove through downtown Atlanta. She stopped and bought a card and a bunch of daffodils before reaching the hospital. She went to the information desk to find out what room to go to. No matter how much was spent on interior design, hospitals seemed depressing. When she reached the room, she knocked lightly on the partially closed door before walking in.

Wanda smiled when she saw Holly standing at the door and closed the magazine she was reading. "Come on in," she said, as she rose from the overstuffed chair beside the empty hospital bed.

"Hi," Holly said, walking across the room to give Wanda a hug. "Where's Carmen?"

"In there." She pointed to the closed bathroom door.

"How's she doing?"

"Okay. I . . ." Wanda paused when the door opened and Carmen walked out.

Carmen looked like she was twelve, not sixteen. She was just shy of five feet and weighed less than a hundred pounds. The light blue hospital gown fit like a tent around her. She smiled when she saw Holly.

"Hey. Are those for me?" She pointed to the flowers Holly was holding.

"Yep. How are you feeling?" Holly hugged her and helped her back to her bed.

"Fine, but I'm sick of this place." Carmen settled in the bed. "And I'm tired of pudding for breakfast, pudding for lunch, and soup for dinner. What I would give for a hamburger."

"You must be feeling better if you're complaining about the food," Wanda said dryly.

Carmen made a face at her sister, then said to Holly, "The only good thing that's happened is that I got a chance to talk to Michael Williams on the telephone Friday."

"Oh, really?"

"Yes. He's really, really nice. He said that we had tickets reserved for his show when I got well." Carmen beamed as she restated her conversation with Mike word for word. He had a fan for life, Holly thought. "He said he would come and see me when he got a chance."

Why did he have to be so nice? Trey wouldn't have thought to call a child in the hospital, much less promise to come for a visit.

"How was the show Friday?" Wanda asked, when Carmen wound down.

"It was great. I think everybody had a good time."

"I heard that you had an especially good time," Wanda said sarcastically.

Holly felt heat rush to her face. She shouldn't feel embarrassed, but she was. She and Mike hadn't tried to hide that fact that they were going out. She knew that Wanda, like the rest of her close friends, would be curious about the first date she'd gone out on since her engagement.

The arrival of a hospital worker with Carmen's lunch diverted Wanda's attention and saved Holly from responding to her comment.

"I'd better go and let you have your lunch," Holly said, as she eased toward the door.

"Some lunch, it's pudding *again*," she said in disgust.

Holly said goodbye and left the hospital. She didn't handle Wanda's statement well. If she was going to see Mike, she would have to get used to the questions and remarks about them.

Why shouldn't she go out? She wasn't engaged anymore. Did people expect her to have no personal life at all? Admittedly, she wasn't a party animal, but she did like to go out every once in a while.

She'd never gone out with someone like Mike. With him, she forgot to be shy. If she wasn't careful, he would make her forget many things, like her plans to move to Seattle. She couldn't let anything alter her plans, not even her growing attraction to Mike.

When she arrived home, she checked for messages on her answering machine. Mike had called her twice. His voice sounded sexy on the tape. "Hi, Holly. It's Mike. Give me a call at work when you get a chance." He left his office number. The next call came an hour later. "Holly, this is Mike. I just wanted to talk to you, but I guess you're not there. Give me a call. I'm still at work."

Holly rewound the tape. He just wanted to talk to her. If it was a line, it had worked. That message made her feel wanted, needed. She picked up the phone and dialed his office.

"Hello." His voice was smooth and deep.

"It's Holly. What are you doing at work on Sunday?"

"Getting ready for work on Monday. What have you been up to?"

"I went to see Carmen at the hospital. You've got a fan for life with her."

"She sounds like a nice kid. How's she doing?"

"Okay, from what I could tell. It was really sweet of you to tell her that you'd come to see her."

"I'm going to go by after I finish here . . . hold on a second."

Holly heard the sound of another man's voice over the phone. Then Mike came back to the phone.

"I've got to take care of this, Holly. I'll call you later tonight, okay?"

"Okay."

Holly put down the phone. She had plenty to do around her house to occupy her time, but she had a feeling that she would be watching the clock until Mike called her tonight. Instead of staying in the house, she decided to visit her grandmother. Grandma Nola always complained that her grandchildren didn't visit her enough.

Mike hung up the phone, unaware of the smile on his face. Thoughts of Holly stayed on his mind while he should have been working on his show. At the sound of someone knocking at his door, he pushed aside thoughts of Holly.

Diane walked into his office. He listened as Andy and Diane discussed the character of what was supposed to be one of his guests on Monday's show.

"I can't believe she canceled because her astrologer said the planets weren't in sync for her tomorrow night," Diane said in disgust.

"This isn't the first time that flake has canceled at the last minute," Andy said, flipping through the pages of his datebook. "Last year she canceled because she went to her renaming ceremony in Las Vegas."

"What?" Diane asked.

"The lady is really strange. She joined this new religious group and everybody had to change his

name. They couldn't just say, 'My name is now so
and so.' Their leader had to perform the ceremony
and *he* picked out their new names."

Mike shook his head in puzzlement and asked,
"Who do we have as a backup for the show?"

"Well, I called the new quarterback of the Falcons
when our other guest called to cancel. He's pretty
popular since he scored the winning touchdown for
the Falcons in the Superbowl, and he wants to be
on the show."

"Good, invite him." Mike shifted his gaze to Diane. "Make sure that the crew knows that he's to
be treated like a king when he's here. If it's not
illegal, immoral, or outrageously expensive, get it
for him."

"Consider it done."

"As of now, Sherylynn is *not* to be invited on the
show again. She's too unreliable," he said, and then
asked his assistant, "Is there anything else on the
schedule that we need to handle?"

"Should I try to get Holly Aimes as a guest?"
Andy asked.

"No!" Diane and Andy looked at him in surprise
at his tone. "No," Mike said again in a quieter voice.
"She's not to be asked to be on the show."

He missed the look that Diane and Andy shared.
Mike had never ruled anyone out as a guest— until
now.

Later that night, Mike walked out on the stage.
When the band played the last note of his theme
song, he began his monologue.

"How many people are into astrology?" A few
members of the audience clapped. "My first guest,

well, she was *supposed* to be my first guest, is also into astrology. But she couldn't be here tonight. Her astrologer said her planets were out of alignment and tonight wouldn't be a good night for her to work. Now," Mike waited for the laughter from the audience to die down.

"Now, I can see me going to the owner of TTN, saying: 'Mr. Thomas, my astrologer said my planets are out of sync and I can't work today.' I wouldn't be working at this network for long. But anyway, Sherylynn couldn't be with us in body, but she can be with us in spirit."

Mike walked to the edge of the stage, where one of his crew members unrolled a life-sized poster of the absent entertainer. "Those of you who clapped earlier when I asked if you were into astrology can verify what I'm about to say. How many of you out there are Geminis?" A few people in the audience clapped.

He reached behind the poster and picked up a book. "According to a noted astrologer, Geminis are detached and inconsiderate. Inconsiderate, hmm. We know *that* applies to Sherylynn. It says here that they make far more promises than they ever keep and repeatedly prove themselves to be totally undependable, self-centered, and insensitive. Folks, all that's in the first paragraph of the chapter on Gemini. I wish I'd read this book before I asked her to appear on the show."

Mike closed the book and put it behind the poster again. "Now, all you fans of Sherylynn, don't get mad with me because I'm being mean to your girl. This isn't the first time she's canceled on us. Diane," he looked up at the control booth. "Why did she cancel the last time?"

"Because her new spiritual leader, Abdul, was performing a renaming ceremony. She had to go to find out what her new name was going to be."

"That's right. She wanted to be called Moonwave for about three months. Let's give Sherylynn or Moonwave her own special seat in the house." He pointed to the very back of the studio. "Put her back there, guys."

The audience applauded as a member of his crew moved the poster. When the applause died down, Mike finished his dialogue.

"As most of you know, proceeds for tonight's show go to one of my favorite charities, Egelston Children's Hospital. Some of the people in the audience are doctors, nurses, and former patients at the hospital. Stand up, guys."

Holly sat glued to her television screen. She watched as his guests donated their time and money to the hospital. She was especially touched when he showed a film clip of his visit to the hospital with members of the Atlanta Hawks basketball team.

He really is a nice man, she thought. When she went to bed that night, she dreamed of him.

As Monday mornings went, this one was the pits, Holly thought. She was late for work because she'd spent thirty minutes trying to decide what to wear. She'd ended up wearing a royal purple suit that her grandmother had given her as a birthday present last year. She had never worn the suit until today.

She told herself that she wasn't dressing up for Mike, but she had thought that if he did call her, she would be dressed for just about anything.

When she arrived at her office, she began reading the *Atlanta Journal*. It was then that she saw the picture. The grainy black-and-white photograph of her and Mike was only an eighth of a page in size, but fear and dread wrapped around her like kudzu in an open field. She placed her cup of tea on her desk and read the print. At least the caption under it wasn't negative. There were a short blurb about Mike's talk show and a brief mention of her engagement to Trey, and her father's bid for reelection was also mentioned.

At least they didn't write a sensational article bringing up the details of her engagement to Trey and his quick marriage, she thought, as she studied the picture. It was not a bad picture of them. The photographer had caught them as they'd watched the children playing soccer in the park. Mike's arms were wrapped around her, and she had a content expression on her face. The embrace suggested that they were sharing a special moment together.

With a quick flip of her wrist, she folded the paper and placed it in the already-read pile on her desk. She could imagine the crowd of reporters firing questions at her, crowding her as she walked to her car. She should have known that going out with Mike would be bad for her, like the death-by-chocolate dessert she indulged in occasionally. Mike had given her pleasure and a high that lasted longer than sugar.

"I don't believe it." Pam walked into Holly's office, staring at Holly with amazement. "Robyn was right— you are wearing something other than black, brown, gray, or navy blue."

"Very funny," Holly muttered.

Pam stood beside her desk. "Stand up so that I see you."

"Go away."

"Not a chance. This is a once-in-a-lifetime event, and I want to make sure that I get the full effect."

"I was wearing pink Friday."

"True," Pam folded her arms. "But I picked out that dress. You chose this by yourself . . . or did you?"

"What kind of question is that?" Holly frowned at her partner.

Pam shrugged her shoulders. "Just asking. Don't get all huffy." She walked around the desk and stood beside Holly's chair. "Anything interesting in the paper?"

Holly tensed and waited for Pam to spot the picture.

"Hmm, nice picture. I take it you had a good time Friday night?"

"Yes, I had a nice time."

"From that picture, it looks like you had more than just a 'nice' time. You don't usually show affection in public because of pictures like this."

Holly remained silent. What Pam said was true. She had an unwritten rule that displays of affection were always done in private. With Mike, she hadn't just bent the rule, she had broken it into tiny pieces.

"For what it's worth, Holly, I'm glad you're going out with Mike. You deserve some happiness after these last few months." The sincere expression on Pam's face warmed her heart. For all the wisecracks and teasing Pam subjected her to, Pam truly cared.

"Thanks." Holly blinked rapidly. She wasn't going to cry. Taking a deep breath, she looked down at the newspaper, then folded it neatly. "Was there something you wanted, or are you just here to give me a hard time?"

Before Pam could answer, the telephone rang.

"Hello. Holly Aimes speaking."

"Good morning, Holly Aimes."

"Hi, Mike." She wasn't able to keep the warmth out of her voice. Pam raised her eyebrows at the tone. Holly felt heat rush to her face and tried to ignore her.

"Have you seen the paper this morning?"

"Yes, I saw it." Holly stared pointedly at Pam. Pam looked at her innocently and made no move to leave.

"What did you think about it?"

"Uhmm . . ." She struggled to think of something that wouldn't give away the conversation. Frowning at Pam, she pointed to her door.

"Holly." Mike's voice sounded smooth and rich, like melted chocolate.

"Hold on a second. I need to get Pam out of my office."

"If you're busy, I can call back later."

"No, Pam is just being nosy."

"I resent that," Pam huffed.

Mike laughed and said, "Tell Pam I said hello."

"Here, you can tell her." Holly punched the button for the speakerphone and put down the handset. "I just put you on the speakerphone."

"Hello, Pam," Mike said, with laughter in his voice.

"Hi there. What did you do to Holly?"

"Pam," Holly said, and gave Pam an I'll-kill-you-if-you-say-anything-to-embarrass-me look.

"What do you mean?" he asked.

"She's wearing new clothes and has a different hairstyle."

"Pam, don't you have work to do?" Holly said, hoping to distract the conversation from its current course.

"Oh yeah. What's she got on?"

"She's got on this sexy purple suit. The skirt ends just above her knees, showing off her legs."

"Pam, get out of my office," Holly snapped.

She continued as if Holly hadn't spoken. ". . . And she's wearing her hair down." Mike's laughter flowed from the telephone. "Ya'll must have a date or something tonight," Pam asked in a teasing tone.

"No," he said in amusement. "Now that you mention it, that's why I called. Are you busy tonight, Holly?"

"She's not doing a thing," Pam blurted.

"Excuse me a second, Mike. I have to kill someone." Holly glared at her partner.

"I'm going, I'm going. 'Bye, Mike." Pam walked out of her office and closed the door behind her.

"Sorry about that. Pam can be bossy at times."

"That's okay. Are you doing anything tonight? I really would like to see you."

How could she resist him when he said things like that? She didn't want to resist. "I'm not doing anything tonight." Or any other night that you ask, she thought.

"Why don't you come to my house for dinner? I think that after the picture in the paper today, we wouldn't be able to go anywhere and have a quiet dinner."

"That's fine. Should I bring anything?"

"Just yourself. I'll see you tonight, around seven?"

"Seven's fine."

"Oh, Holly, don't change. I'd like to see that sexy purple suit." He hung up before she could answer him.

Mike smiled and leaned back in the soft leather chair in his home office. Holly hadn't refused to go out, despite the picture in the newspaper. That had been his one fear, but she had agreed to come to his house for dinner. Now all he had to do was tell the new chef to make dinner for two.

His smile melted when he looked at the note on his desk. Trey Christian had agreed to appear on his show Thursday. He didn't know how she would take the news.

He pushed aside the guilt he felt. He had never had to consider the feelings of others when he'd interviewed a guest— until Holly. She had to know that he wouldn't do anything to deliberately hurt her. There was no use in worrying about it now. He'd take one day at a time, one problem at a time.

* * *

Holly couldn't concentrate. She closed the file she had been staring at for the past thirty minutes. It was useless. She wasn't going to accomplish anything today. Mike and their date tonight dominated her thoughts. She couldn't wait to see him, to experience his kiss, to feel the warm strength of his arms wrapped around her. The memory of the kiss they'd shared Saturday caused heat to spread throughout her body. Holly looked at the clock on her desk, willing the time to pass quickly. It didn't.

She left her office at six o'clock and a reporter met her by the front entrance of the office building.

"Miss Aimes." The short, stocky man pointed a microphone in front of her face. "May I ask you some questions?"

Holly froze for a second, then walked quickly past him. "I'm not going to answer questions," she said purposefully.

The reporter continued to walk beside her. "Are you seeing Michael Williams?"

"No comment." Holly increased the stride to a brisk trot.

The reporter fell back a few steps, but ran to catch up with her. "What do you think about the separation of Trey Christian and his wife?"

That question surprised her. She hadn't heard about that, and she didn't want to know. Holly reached her car, opened the door, and started the engine. She hoped the reporter didn't know what he was talking about concerning Trey and his wife, but a part of her hoped it was true. It would serve Trey right if his wife left him. Holly smiled as she thought of Trey experiencing the pain and embarrassment he'd put her through.

She turned on the radio and sang along. Her day was suddenly a little brighter. As she moved with the early evening rush hour, she thought of the night ahead with Mike. She couldn't imagine him ever running off and marrying another woman, leaving his fiancée to face the press alone. He had too much pride and honesty to do something like that.

The sun cast a golden glow on his house. She parked her car and walked to the door. Mike was waiting there.

"Hi," he said.

"Hello."

"Now that we've got that over with." He pulled her into his arms and kissed her. The kiss was hot and wet and conveyed his need for her. His fingers tangled her hair, cupping her head as if to hold her captive, but Holly had no desire whatsoever to leave his embrace. His tongue teased hers with long, slow strokes.

Abruptly he tore his lips from hers and leaned his forehead against hers. His chest moved in and out as if he couldn't get enough air.

"I've been waiting to do that all day long." His voice was husky with desire.

Holly marveled that she could affect him so much. She struggled to catch her breath and tighten her arms around his waist. It felt so good to hold him like this.

"Dinner, you came to eat dinner." He released her from his embrace and stepped aside to allow her to enter his home. "I hope you're hungry," he said, as they walked to the dining room.

The dining room table was set for two. A fresh fruit salad was artfully arranged on salad plates.

"Did you get a new chef?" Holly asked, as Mike helped her to her chair.

"Yes, a young guy named Henry. Not *Henri,*" he said in a heavy French accent, "just plain Henry. He wanted to make that point very clear when I interviewed him." Mike sat in the chair across from her. "He's good . . . so far."

"Good. I don't want you to go hungry."

The look that he gave her made her mouth go dry. The heat and passion in his eyes singed her heart. "I'm always hungry when I'm with you."

She had no defenses left. The raw, primitive desire inside her burned deep and all thought of food vanished from her mind. The air in the room seemed thick and heavy. She could barely draw enough oxygen in her lungs and she fought to catch her breath. Mike's passionate gaze traveled from her eyes to her cheeks to her trembling lips. She felt as if he had touched each spot that his gaze had caressed.

He lowered his lids, releasing her from the sensual spell.

"You shouldn't say things like that," she said, her voice husky with desire.

"Why not? It's true. I *am* hungry when I'm with you. You're very sexy, and I'd like nothing better than to make love to you."

"I know that I'm not sexy. You don't have to say

things like that to me. I've known for a long time that I'm not special to look at."

Mike looked at her. She could still see the banked passion in his eyes. "We'll agree to disagree, but for now, let's just enjoy dinner."

Holly reached for the salad fork with trembling fingers. She pierced a fresh strawberry and took a bite. There was silence in the room while they ate. Why did she have to argue with him, she thought. Why didn't she just take the compliment in stride, even if she knew it wasn't true? She pierced another piece of fruit and ate it, keeping her eyes on the salad plate.

"How did your day go today?" Mike asked. Holly mentally sighed in relief. He was dropping the subject. She told him about the mix-ups at work and how it had been a typical Monday. They kept the subject of conversation general throughout dinner. When Mike placed a slice of chocolate cheesecake in front of her, she groaned.

"I shouldn't be eating this," she said, picking up her fork.

"It's just one piece. It can't hurt you," he said, before taking a bite.

They ate the sinfully rich dessert in silence. Holly turned down his offer of coffee and followed him into the den. "I don't think I could take in another thing. Tell Henry he did an excellent job," she said, as she sat on the overstuffed sofa.

"That dinner is going to make me almost useless at work tonight." Mike sat next to her. His long legs stretched out in front of him.

"What time do you have to be there?"

"Ten o'clock." He looked at his watch. "That gives us two hours."

A lot could happen in two hours, she thought. Mike reached for her hand.

"I know that I didn't tell you this earlier, but you look lovely tonight."

"Thank you. It's the suit." She gestured to her purple outfit.

"No. I don't think it's the suit. It's you."

Holly tugged her hand away from his. "I told you that you don't have to say things like that to me. I'm well aware of how I look."

Mike shook his head, then stood up. "Come here." He held out his hand to her. She placed her hand in his and moved from the sofa. He led her to a large mirror across the room. Standing behind her, he put his hands on her shoulders. "Look in the mirror, Holly." He took his hands off her shoulders and moved her hair off her shoulder, leaving her neck vulnerable. Slowly, he smoothed the back of his hand from the base of her neck to her chin. She watched his actions in the beveled mirror, shivering at the sensual expression visible on his face.

"I don't know why you think you're not sexy," he whispered. "Your skin is so soft. I want to touch each and every part of your body." His eyes met hers in the mirror. Leisurely he lowered his lips to her neck. His teeth caught her skin, then his tongue soothed the small bite.

She watched as he slid the collar of her jacket aside and he kissed her shoulder once, then twice. His hand went to her shoulders, then traveled lazily down her arms. Nuzzling her neck, he carried her hands to her waist with his arms surrounding her. His fingers entwined with hers briefly before he released his grip. He pressed his body against hers. She could feel the strong proof of his desire and the rapid movement of his chest. His hands moved from her waist slowly upward. Holly held her breath when his hand gently cupped her breast. Softly, like the wings of a butterfly, his thumb brushed her nipple. She heard a harsh sound and realized that she was making the noise. She closed her eyes when he circled her nipple with his thumb.

"You are so beautiful," he said, his breath brushing against her neck. His hands made short work of the buttons in front of her jacket. She tensed when he opened the jacket. "Don't, Holly. I want to see you."

Watching, he opened her jacket, revealing soft, brown skin and breasts barely covered by a skimpy navy lace bra.

"Oh God, sweet. Oh God," he cried. With trembling hands he unfastened the hooks at her back and pushed the thin bra straps and the jacket down her arms.

"Perfect," he said, as he cupped her breasts. "So perfect."

She placed her hands over his and squeezed. His callused hands felt wonderful against her. She leaned against him, letting his hands wander across her chest. He turned her around to face him. He spread open-mouthed kisses upon her face before devouring her lips. He was like a thirsty man who had come upon a cool spring. He kept kissing her as if he couldn't get enough of her. He fell to his knees before her, kissing the smooth skin on her torso. He wrapped his arms around her hips and pressed his face against her. He caressed her hips and moved his hand down her thighs until he reached the hem of her skirt.

She looked down and met his gaze. She felt his hands move under her skirt and travel up her thighs. His eyes widened when he reached the top of her stockings and felt her bare flesh. He paused to caress her thighs before moving up and pulling her lace panties down her thighs, past her knees, and finally, to her feet. She stepped out of them.

Her knees became like water when his hands traveled up her legs and touched the soft hair that covered her femininity. He guided her down on her knees to the carpet beside him, then edged her down farther until she lay on her back.

He leaned down until his chest covered hers, taking most of his weight on his elbows. Their legs entwined and he pressed his hips against hers. "I want you. Let me give you pleasure." Then he kissed her. Her arms wrapped around his shoulders and she could feel the soft silk of his shirt. He lowered his head and suckled one nipple while his hand milked the other. She felt as if she were drowning. Wave after wave of longing flowed through her body.

"Mike, Mike," she cried. Her fingers clutched at his shoulders. He left her breast and kissed her stomach, his hand pushing her skirt up her legs until he uncovered the soft black hair that shielded her. She made a wild crooning noise when his fingers raked through her shield and found the small nub. Gently, ever so gently, he touched her. Her hips bucked wildly against his hand. He lowered his head again to her breast and suckled. He kissed, stroked, and touched her body with a single-minded intent. Holly felt as if her body was being ravished with pleasure. He whispered raw, sensual phrases of desire, encouraging her to let go, telling her how beautiful she looked to him. Tears filled her eyes as she raced to that height of desire. Then it happened. She reached the pinnacle of satisfaction and desire.

He felt her body tense, then heard the sweet cry of her release. He almost lost it then. He looked down at her face. She looked as if she were in the most exquisite pain, but the tremors from her body spoke of the pleasure she'd received.

He kissed away the tears that streamed down her face and gentled her until the shaking stopped. He felt as if he could conquer the world. He never thought that he could receive so much pleasure by giving pleasure to another, and that was exactly what happened tonight. He kissed her trembling lips and stroked her hair away from her face. Black lashes formed half-moons on her cheeks. He kissed her eyelids and rolled them both to the side.

Slowly, she opened her eyes and looked at him.

"You're beautiful, you're sexy, and from this night on, you're mine."

Eight

She was floating on a sensual cloud, boneless and weightless. She felt the soft carpet beneath her and the heat of Mike's body beside her. Opening her eyes, she looked at his face, so strong, so handsome. He lay on his side with one hand supporting his head. He watched her and his eyes met hers, dark and filled with desire.

"You, you didn't . . ." Her voice trailed off as she stared helplessly into his eyes.

He reached down and brought her wrist to his lips. He kissed the soft, silky skin and felt the rapid beat of her pulse. He spread kisses from her wrist to the middle of her palm. "Tonight is just for you, sweet," he said, placing her hand beside her head.

"Mike?"

"Shh." His fingers brushed her lips. "Let me give you pleasure tonight."

She groaned. "I don't think I can take any more pleasure."

Mike's smile was wicked and sexy and promised her the world. "A woman's body is capable of abundant pleasure." He proceeded to prove it to her.

* * *

For the first time in his career, Mike was almost late for work. He usually arrived at the studio a couple of hours ahead of time, but tonight, he had only ten minutes to review the list of questions he had for each guest. But it was worth it.

He smiled as he remembered carrying an exhausted Holly upstairs to his bed. He doubted she'd remember him removing her purple skirt, shoes, and stockings. He, on the other hand, would never forget the sight of her nude body lying on his bed. The groan that tore from his lips caused her to stir in the bed.

She was beautiful— achingly, wonderfully beautiful. His gaze feasted over her body from her long graceful legs, over her rounded, shapely hips, up her flat, firm stomach, to her full breasts, along her graceful neck, to her full lips, which were slightly parted. Her high, exotic cheeks were fanned by long black lashes. Her shoulder-length black hair spread out on the pillow beneath her head.

How could she possibly think that she wasn't sexy? He felt a sharp wave of desire spread down to his groin. He turned and walked to his bathroom. As he shed his clothes, he turned on the shower. The cold blast of water took the edge off his desire. He would like to get his hands on Trey Christian and strangle him if he was responsible for the self-doubt that Holly had about her sexuality. With a sharp twist, he turned off the shower and toweled dry. He quickly put on his clothes and walked out of the bathroom.

Holly lay on her stomach, one leg bent and one hand under her cheek. He spread a lightweight blanket over her and kissed her cheek. Long lashes fluttered and she barely opened her eyes.

"Go back to sleep, sweetheart. I'll see you when I get home." He watched as her eyes closed once again and she burrowed beneath the blanket.

"One minute, Mike." The voice of his assistant, Andy Kurtz, broke through the pleasant memory. Mike stood from his desk and walked to the door where Andy stood. They walked quickly through the back of the studio.

Bright lights followed his path as he walked out on the stage. As the applause died down, he looked out into the crowd.

"How many people out there work full-time?" The majority raised their hands. "Now, how many of you would like to run the company that you work for?" Most of the hands stayed up. "How many of you think that you could run the company better than it's being run now?"

Mike looked over the crowd and spotted his cameraman with her hand raised. "Wait a minute. Move the camera over here." He walked to the cameraman. "Come on down here." The audience laughed when they realized it was one of his crew.

"You think you can do a better job than me, running this show?"

"Yeah."

"Well, ain't that a blip?"

"Of course, it would be called the Brenda Reese Show."

"Oh, you want me totally out of the show?"

"No; you can run the camera."

"Get back up there. My own people want me

gone. I've got to rethink letting them run the show on Friday."

"Oh, no, you don't." A voice came from the sound deck. "You said we could run the show Friday, and we're going to run it."

"That's the producer, Diane," he laughed, then said, "I guess I don't have a choice. Seriously, on Friday the crew gets to run the show for a day. I have no say in the format— or anything else, it seems. This ought to be interesting."

"You just get here on time," Diane said.

"Do you hear this?" He looked out into the crowd. "I wasn't late, just a little behind schedule."

"You were late."

"Okay, once in five years I wasn't here at least an hour early, and now I'm late. I walked out on the stage on time." Mike said to the audience, "Somebody, tell me what time it is." Someone yelled out the time. "See? I'm right on schedule, Diane."

"Just don't let it happen again."

"Rough crowd tonight."

Holly slowly opened her eyes. The bed didn't feel familiar. Why was she sleeping without her gown? Pale beams of moonlight filled the room, making the room look surreal, almost fairylike. She sat up in bed. The blanket fell to her waist. That was when she saw Mike sitting in the shadows of the room.

A single beam of light illuminated his face. She could tell from the way he lounged in the chair that he had been watching her for a long time. Silently, he rose from the chair and walked to the bed.

Holly reached for the blanket to cover her breasts. She was so embarrassed. She had never given herself to anyone but Trey, and she had only made love with him after they'd become engaged.

"Don't do that, Holly." He reached for the blanket.

"I should go home." She looked down at the hand tugging on the blanket. Mortified, she realized that she didn't know where her clothes were. "Please, I've got to leave." Tears welled in her eyes.

"Look at me." He touched her chin and sat on the edge of the bed. Through the tears, she saw his handsome face filled with warmth and desire. "Don't ever feel embarrassed about what we shared tonight. There's nothing to be ashamed of."

She looked into his eyes and her embarrassment faded away when she saw the honesty in his face. "I really should go home." She looked away.

Silence filled the room. "On one condition," he said, and waited until she looked at him. "I want to see you tomorrow. We can go out or have a quiet night at your house, but either way, I want to see you."

"I want to see you, but I don't know if I can give you what you want, Mike. I don't sleep around, and tonight . . ."

"We'll take it one night at a time. But Holly, we *will* become lovers." He stood beside the bed and gestured to the set of double doors. "Your clothes are in the closet. I'll wait for you downstairs."

Holly threw off the blanket and rushed to the closet when he closed the door behind him. She couldn't believe that she'd let him do the things he'd done tonight. What was more unbelievable was the fact that she'd enjoyed every minute of it.

She spotted her clothes the minute she opened the closet doors. Her feminine suit looked out of place among the rows of heavier masculine suits. She felt heat rush to her cheeks as she imagined him collecting each of her discarded garments from the floor, carrying them upstairs, and carefully placing them on a hanger. Her stockings, bra and panties were draped over another hanger.

She nearly put a run in her stocking as she hurriedly dressed. She stepped into her shoes, which were neatly placed between a pair of black wingtips and some burgundy loafers. When she was finally dressed, she left his bedroom.

Mike sat on the stairs. When he heard the door open, he stood.

Her legs felt like rubber. She didn't think they would support her as she walked down the stairs.

"Well, I guess I'll be going," she said, when she reached the last stair. She raised her gaze briefly to his chin, unable to look him in the eye before lowering her head.

"We need to talk." She was shaking her head "no" before he finished the sentence. Mike stared at her in frustration. Her body language was unwelcoming, her head was bent, and her shoulders were rolled forward. He knew then that she wouldn't remain in his presence any longer.

"I'll follow you home." He reached out, touching her arm.

"You don't have to." She stepped back until he no longer touched her. "I'll be fine."

"I'll follow you home. I can't have you driving around town this late at night."

He followed her to her house. She felt safe, knowing that he followed her through the dark, empty streets of Atlanta. They drove down the deserted street to her house. He parked his car behind hers and walked her to the front door.

"Thanks for following me home." She put the key into the lock. She felt his fingers on her chin. She looked up at him. Inch by inch he lowered his head. The kiss was sweet, soft, and nonthreatening. "Goodnight, sweet. I'll see you tomorrow."

Holly didn't regret what she and Mike had shared last night. It was just unnerving to learn that after years of believing that she was plain, the sexiest black man in America found her attractive.

She took time with her makeup this morning and paused to really look at herself. Warm brown skin stretched over high cheeks; her eyes tilted up at the edges. Overall, she didn't look bad.

When she arrived at her office, the same reporter waited as she walked to the door. She ignored him and walked inside the lobby. Robyn and Pam did a double take when she walked in the door.

"Two days in a row," Pam said in amazement, when she saw Holly dressed in a bright red pantsuit. "Is there snow predicted in the weather forecast?"

"Stuff it, Pam. Good morning, Robyn."

"Good morning, Holly." Robyn said. "I like your suit."

"Thank you." Holly picked up her mail and headed down the hall to her office.

"Wait just a minute." Pam walked after her. "This must be serious. I've never seen you like this."

"Like what?"

"Like this." Pam waved her hand toward Holly. "You're dressing to attract attention. You didn't do that when you were engaged to Bozo."

"I like this," Holly said, as she sat in her chair, dropping her mail on her desk.

"Hello. Remember me? The woman who knows you." Pam looked at Holly with a serious expression on her face. "I don't want to see you hurt, Holly."

"You're the one who encouraged me to go out with Mike."

"I know, but I didn't think you'd change. You're really beginning to care for him, aren't you?"

Holly took her time in answering. "Yes, I care for him."

"What about Seattle? Are you still planning to move?"

"Yes, I'm still planning to move. Our relationship is just temporary. He knows I plan to move soon."

"You're not the temporary-relationship type. Can you move knowing that you care for him?"

Holly lifted her chin at a stubborn angle. "Yes, I can."

Pam looked at her with skepticism. "I don't believe you can. I think you're fooling yourself if you think you can." Pam held her gaze for a long, uncomfortable moment before she walked out of Holly's office.

Holly frowned. Could she leave him? Couldn't she? She wanted to believe she could. She had to leave. She knew that she couldn't stand another round with the press when their relationship ended . . . and it *would* end. Looking at her desk, she spotted the crystal container full of candy kisses. She took off the top and selected a piece. She would have to treat their relationship like she did chocolate. As much as she wanted to, she couldn't have it whenever she wanted without paying the price. The price of caring for Mike Williams was more than she could afford.

Holly pushed that thought aside and began to work. She would take care that she didn't get hurt and enjoy her time with him.

She told herself that she was buying the sexy underwear for herself. But deep down inside, she knew that she was buying it for Mike. She had already gone to the drugstore to buy protection for both of them. There was no denying that she wanted to make love to Mike.

She still was embarrassed at the way she had responded to him last night. Seeing their reflection in the mirror had aroused her more than she could ever believe. She wandered through the lunchtime crowd at the suburban shopping mall. She felt happier today than she had in a long time, freer somehow. Making her way back to the parking lot, she smiled because for the first time she felt attractive. Not the unmistakable beauty her sister was, but pretty, and maybe even a little sexy. With a bounce in her step, she walked to her car and drove back to her office.

The ringing telephone interrupted Holly's concentration. Annoyed, she picked up the phone. "Hello, Holly Aimes."

"Hi, I'm calling to tempt you." Mike's voice was husky, smooth, and sexy.

It wouldn't take much, she thought to herself. "What have you got in mind?" she asked, leaning back in her chair.

"How would you like to join me at the studio today? A group of musicians are practicing for tonight's show."

"Well . . . I don't know. I've got lots to do today."

"You know you really don't want to work on such a pretty day. We could listen to them play for a little while, then we could go outside and play ourselves. No work, no phones, nothing."

Holly looked at the folders on her desk, then turned to look out her window. The sun was shining brightly and the day was indeed pretty. Work could wait. She wanted to be with Mike more than she wanted to work.

"I could be persuaded to leave early. What time should I meet you?" she asked, looking at her watch.

"How about right now?"

Holly arrived at the studios of Thomas Television Network. Mike had left her name at the guard station and she was allowed to enter the gates. She saw Mike the instant she walked inside the building. He was dressed in baggy jeans and a casual short-sleeved shirt that showed off his muscular arms. Her heart quickened in her chest when he smiled at her.

"I'm glad you came," he said, and guided her to a bank of elevators.

"I didn't need much encouragement to leave today." She walked inside the elevator car. They were the only two people on board. The doors closed. Mike pulled her against his body and kissed her, quick, hard, and thoroughly. He released her moments before the doors to the elevator opened and two men in suits entered.

Holly struggled to regain her composure. Kissing Mike was like drinking brandy: strong, smooth, and potent.

They exited the elevator on the fourth floor, walking down the carpeted hallway until they reached glass double doors that read, "Williams Production, Inc." Mike used a card key to release the locks and held open the door for her to enter. They walked past the receptionist, who was busy with phone calls, but she took time to wave to them as they passed.

They came to a door at the end of the hallway. Mike reached for the doorknob and turned to her. "Don't let these guys intimidate you." He opened the door before she could question him.

They entered the studio where she had sat last Friday. It should have seemed empty, but the group of people milling around the band stage made enough noise to make the studio seem full. The mingling of voices warming up and the directions for mike check created an air of confusion.

"Hey, guys," Mike called out to the group. The voices died down and everyone turned to look at them.

Holly gasped when she recognized the internationally known artist. Mike smiled down at her.

"I want you guys to meet Holly Aimes."

A chorus of "hellos" greeted her. "Holly is playing hooky from work, and I invited her over to hear you practice before the show."

"Come over here with us, Holly." The singer gestured her toward the group. She was introduced to everyone from the backup singers to the musicians. Everyone was friendly and joked around until it was time to practice. Then the laughter stopped and serious work started. Mike led her to the first row of the empty studio. For the next hour they listened to music that could only be heard at a live concert. Sitting beside her, Mike put his arm around her, clearly demonstrating to everyone in the studio that they were a couple.

When the musicians finished their practice, she watched as Mike interacted with the group as if they were old friends.

"Hi again."

Mike's producer, Diane, sat in the row behind her.

"Hi."

"They're great, aren't they?"

"Yes. I've never seen them in concert. This was great."

They fell silent as they looked at the group.

"You know, Mike has never brought anyone to the studio, other than his family. You must be very special to him." Diane stood and left. Holly watched her walk across the studio to join the group.

She had to be mistaken, Holly thought. She couldn't be that important to him, could she? She was just a convenient date to him. But even as Holly denied Diane's statement, hope sprang within her. Holly looked at the group and smiled when Mike motioned her over. I'm not going to hope, she told herself.

She would be moving soon, and from what she'd heard, long-distance relationships didn't work out well. No, she thought, walking to the group, she wouldn't hope. She would enjoy the time they had together and concentrate on opening a new branch office in Seattle.

"Hey, you don't want to hang around this guy," the singer said, when she reached Mike's side. "Why don't you meet me after the show?" He wiggled his eyebrows jokingly. "I'll treat you better than he will."

"She's mine. Get your own girl." Mike put his arms around her as if to hold her back from the singer.

Everyone laughed at the joke, and for that brief moment, Holly felt like she was his girl.

"We're going to Dave and Buster's. Why don't you come with us?"

"No, we're going to pass this time," Mike said.

The singer smiled at them. "I understand. See you later." He shook Mike's hand and, turning to Holly, took her hand and brushed his lips across

the back of it. "Are you coming to the show tonight?" He continued when she shook her head
"no." "It was a pleasure to meet you, Holly."

Soon the studio was empty except for the two of
them. "Now, wasn't that much better than working?" He took her in his arms. The warmth of his
body filtered through her clothes and wrapped
around her.

"Yes, it was." She put her arms around his waist,
laying her head on his shoulder. "Thank you so
much."

His arms tightened around her, pulling her
closer into his embrace. She savored the masculine
scent that was his and his alone. Against her cheek
she felt the slow, steady beat of his heart.

The sound of voices shattered the silence and
broke the quiet, intimate atmosphere surrounding
them. "Let's go have some fun," he said, and took
her hand.

Mike drove to a movie theater with six screens.
They argued over which movie to see, then decided
to see them both, since they had enough time. Mike
bought a large tub of buttered popcorn and two
Cokes. The theater had less than twenty people seeing the movie. They sat toward the back of the theater, trying to answer the movie trivia that flashed
on the screen. The lights dimmed and the action-
adventure started.

Later that evening, she picked up her car from
the studio and followed him to his house for dinner.
When they reached his home, the smell of fresh-
baked cake sent them to the kitchen. The man
chopping green and red pepper looked like he was

a member of a gang. He was well over six feet tall and solidly muscular. His hair was cut so close that he looked almost bald, and his skin was the color of rich coffee. But it was the brown, penetrating eyes that made her feel as if he could see right through her. That and the fact that he wielded the knife like he could carve a man as well as chop vegetables made her want to give him all the space he needed.

"Henry." The man turned to them. He wasn't smiling. "I'd like you to meet Holly. Holly, this is Henry, the new chef."

Henry nodded to her and turned back to the chopping block.

"Nice to meet you, Henry."

"Ma'am." His voice matched his appearance . . . intimidating.

They left the kitchen and went to the den. "Where on earth did you find him?" she whispered.

"He was recommended by one of my neighbors. The only reason he didn't hire Henry was because he had worked with his chef for five years."

"Doesn't he intimidate you?"

"No. One thing I learned is that how a person looks on the outside has nothing to do with the way he is on the inside. I don't care what he looks like. He cooks the food I like when I like it, no questions asked."

"Would you really complain if *he* served you tofu burger?"

"Yeah, I'd complain . . . over the telephone,

when I was out of town! We've got thirty minutes before Henry serves dinner. Do you play pool?"

"I haven't played in some time."

Mike pick up two pool sticks and offered her one. "How about a game to pass the time? I promise I won't embarrass you too badly when I beat you." He smiled and set up the balls.

Two games later, Mike wasn't smiling. Holly was poised to win the third game. She carefully considered her move. Holly made the last shot and smiled smugly at Mike.

"Dinner is ready, Mr. Williams." Henry stood in the door of the den. She jumped at the sound of Henry's deep, loud voice.

"We'll be right there," Mike said, replacing the cue sticks.

Henry left as quietly as he had arrived.

"I thought you said you hadn't played in some time," Mike asked.

"I haven't played since sometime last week," she said with a frown. "I know who Henry reminds me of . . . Lurch on *The Addams Family*."

Mike looked at her, then smiled. "You know, you're right. Can you image him in a black tuxedo?"

Holly shook her head. "It boggles the mind."

They walked to the dining room, where Henry waited next to the buffet. Holly had a hard time trying not to imagine Henry in a tuxedo.

"We'll serve ourselves tonight, Henry, thank you."

Henry showed no emotion. "Very well, Mr. Williams. I'll see you tomorrow." He walked out of the room.

Holly whispered to Mike, "I think we hurt his feelings by not letting him serve dinner."

"Are you kidding me? He's probably glad I told him to leave." Mike walked to the buffet and surveyed the food. "Grilled salmon, stir-fried vegetables and rice, and for dessert, lemon cake," Mike said, then breathed in the aroma of the food. "Not a single alfalfa sprout, and no tofu."

Holly laughed at him. "Well, don't just stand there. Feed me. I'm hungry." She sat down at the table and waited for him to serve her.

"Yes, dear." Mike made his voice nasally and wimpy, then proceed to serve her dinner.

She took a bite of the fish and closed her eyes in ecstasy. "I'm having dinner here every night and I take back everything I said about Henry. This is wonderful."

"You're welcome to come over every night— for dinner and anything else."

She paused and met his gaze across the table. His eyes spoke of sin and desire. There was no doubt that dinner wasn't the only thing she was welcome to share with him. Desire that had been held at bay surged forward throughout her body. Heat rose and spread from her face to the very center of her.

"Uhmm, thank you." Holly broke the sensual bond and looked down at her plate.

"Holly, you know that I want to make love to you."

She couldn't think of a single reply. A thousand thoughts ran through her mind and all of them were sexually explicit. She had never played the sexual word game before, and now she was right in the middle of the game and didn't know the rules. How could she tell him that she wanted to make love to him right this very minute without sounding like a sex-starved maniac?

She envisioned herself slowly taking off her clothes while he stared in amazement or telling him that now wouldn't be too soon to make love. Instead of doing or saying anything, she ate.

Silence stretched between them and she could almost see the tension in the air. The clang of silverware against the plates and the tinkle of ice shifting in their glasses were the only sounds in the room.

"Mike." Her heart pounded in her chest; her eyes were glued to her plate. "Will you make love to me tonight?"

She could have sworn that the room couldn't have gotten any quieter, but it had. Oh, Lord, he doesn't want to make love to me, she thought. He wasn't serious. When she worked up enough nerve to look across the table, she was nearly burned by the heat and desire in his eyes.

"Are you sure, Holly, because there's no turning back once you say yes."

Holly met his gaze and with a husky, passion-filled voice, she said, "I'm sure."

Ninε

Mike rose from his chair. Instantly he was beside her. Taking her hand, he urged her to her feet. The dinner that they barely touched lay forgotten on the table.

Heat and desire raced through her body as she stared into his molten brown eyes. He wanted her—that much was clear. He slid his arms around her waist to her back, pressing their bodies together.

"Holly." He kissed her cheek, then the corner of her mouth. "Sweet Holly."

She parted her lips and shivered when his tongue slipped inside. With long, slow strokes he mated with her mouth, and with each stroke he created a wave of desire within her that rolled from her breast to the depths of her femininity. He gave her one final mind-numbing kiss before holding her away from him.

"Come with me." He took her hand and led them up the stairs to his bedroom. The early evening sun came through the large windows, giving the room a warm glow. Holly looked at the windows uncertainly. She had always made love in the cover of darkness. In this room she would be exposed. There was no way she could hide.

"Mike."

He turned to her when they reached the bed. He saw the uncertain expression on her face. Tenderness warred with his desire. "Are you having second thoughts?" His voice carried the strain of his emotions.

Holly held her head down, afraid to meet his gaze, afraid to see the anger and frustration he must be feeling.

"Sweet, the last thing I want to do is make you uncomfortable. Tell me what's wrong."

"I . . . I'm nervous."

Mike lifted her chin. "We won't do anything that you're not comfortable doing. We've got all the time in the world." His body would make him pay for that statement. His body made demands that wanted, no, needed to be filled.

He led her to one of the Queen Anne chairs in the room. He sat down, pulling Holly into his lap. She felt his hard and rigid manhood against her hips. She lay her head on his shoulder and his arms wrapped around her. He tilted her chin up and he kissed her with gentle, tender kisses. He kissed her forehead, her eyebrows, her cheeks, and her chin before worrying her lips. He suckled, licked, and gave her little love bites on her lips.

She felt as if she couldn't get enough oxygen in her lungs. His hands wandered from her waist down her hips, stroking her, caressing her. She could feel the rapid beat of his heart when her hands explored his firm chest. She touched him, gliding her hands from the middle of his chest to his broad shoulders. His skin was hot, as if a fire burned within him.

His hands found the small buttons on her shirt and he began to release them one at a time. She sat up as he removed her shirt. The lacy white bra barely covered her breasts. Her dark brown nipples showed through the silky material. He ran his thumb over one nipple and groaned in satisfaction when it puckered against the lace. His hands went to her back and he unhooked the bra, sliding the straps off her arms, slowly revealing her smooth, brown breasts.

Instinctively, she crossed her arms to cover herself, but Mike put his hands over hers and looked into her eyes.

"Holly, don't hide from me. You're beautiful." His eyes were hot with passion and sincerity. "I love looking at your body."

She yielded, letting him move her hands, uncovering her breasts.

With hands that trembled slightly, Mike slid his fingertips on the sides of her breasts. She shivered at the feelings that his touch evoked within her. The shyness was gone and in its place was the yearning to be stroked and caressed. Holding her breath, she watched as he made lazy circles, spanning the circumference of the swell of her breasts. The circles grew smaller and smaller until he outlined her coffee-brown nipple. Then he stroked her with butterfly-light strokes. She released her pent-up breath with a groan. Her action moved her body from his pleasurable hands. She took his hand and placed his palm over her breast and held it there. She arched her back as she pressed his palm harder against her. Yearning desire shone in her eyes as she met his gaze.

Mike brought his other hand up to stroke her, but it wasn't enough; she wanted to touch him. She reached for his shirt and pulled it out of the waistband of his pants. Her fingers trembled as she tried to unbutton his shirt. Their arms tangled as each stroked the other. Finally, Mike joined in the quest to remove his shirt. The cotton shirt was removed quickly, revealing his smooth, muscled chest.

Holly leaned forward. She kissed his chin and slowly spread kisses along his jaw and his neck. She slid out of his lap to kneel between his knees on the carpeted floor. Then she touched her lips to his hard chest. Her hands spread along his sides moving upward, caressing every ripple of his hard waist and under his arms before moving inward across his chest.

His chest was smooth, almost hairless. His muscles jerked in reaction when she touched his small, pebble-like nipples. She looked at him when she stroked him again. His hands moved urgently down her shoulders and arms. Holly leaned forward and kissed the middle of his chest. Mike stiffened and became totally still. Holly looked at his face. His eyes closed and his expression was one of pain.

"Mike?"

His eyes opened. "Do that again," he said in a voice she didn't recognize. She lowered her gaze and kissed him again. She felt the groan that racked his body. His hands moved to the back of her head and his fingers combed through her hair. She kissed every inch of his chest, savoring each and every caress, slowly, ever so slowly, making her way down until she reached his navel. Her tongue flirted with his navel in a gentle game of taste and retreat.

Desire and freedom that she'd never felt before made her bold. She kissed the skin above the waistband of his jeans, then gave him gentle love bites, soothing the bites with a touch of her tongue.

When she slid her hand under the waistband of his jeans, he got out of the chair. He was on his knees beside her in an instant. His mouth devoured hers. She felt the fire when she leaned against him, his hard chest to her breast. As they kissed, he leaned her down until she could feel the carpet beneath her bare back, supporting most of his weight on his forearms. Their legs tangled together and she felt the rigid proof of his desire for her.

The buckle of his belt pressed against her stomach. Holly reached between them, grazing his washboard stomach. Mike moved to lie on his side while she struggled with the belt buckle. Finally, the catch leased on the belt and she unbuttoned the single button of his jeans, then pulled down the zipper tab, revealing white cotton briefs and the bulge of his manhood. Reaching inside, Holly stroked the hot bulge, tearing harsh groans from Mike. She moved over the cotton briefs from the very base of his shaft to his smooth, velvety tip.

Mike reached down and caught her hand. He guided her to the rubber waistband of his briefs. His eyes held hers as he slowly slid her hand underneath the fabric. Holly felt the springy short hair which covered his firm stomach. Inch by inch her hand traveled down his stomach, moving in rhythm with the rise and fall as he breathed deep, rapid breaths.

Then a shrill beeping sound pierced the room. They froze, then looked down at his watch, which was partially covered by the waistband of his briefs.

"Damn!" That one word conveyed all of Mike's frustration. Holly watched the struggle in his face. Anger, frustration, and unmistakable desire showed in his black-brown eyes. Reluctantly, he removed her hand and rolled over on his side with his back to her. Holly struggled to catch her breath as she listened to the steady beep of his watch alarm. Mike turned off the alarm and the silence was broken by the harsh sound of Mike trying to catch his breath.

Holly also struggled to regain calm. The unfulfilled desire throbbed through her body, leaving her waiting and wanting. Confused, she watched Mike rise from the floor and zip his jeans. He straightened his shoulders as if to prepare himself for a difficult battle, then turned to Holly.

The desire and wanting were still visible in his expression, but so was resignation. "I've got to go to work, sweet."

Work? Work. Holly closed her eyes and groaned. She'd totally forgotten about his job. She'd forgotten just about everything but the passionate desire that he seemed to bring out in her. Reluctantly, she opened her eyes again and watched as he reached down to pick up his discarded shirt. She watched his muscles ripple when he put his arms through the shirtsleeves. She looked lower to the still rigid bulge in his pants.

"Stop it, Holly," he said, his voice deepened by desire.

She dragged her gaze back to his face. The passion in his eyes nearly burned her. Holly lowered her gaze and spotted her bra at the foot of the chair. She reached across the floor and picked up the lacy garment. She shivered when the material rubbed her sensitive nipples.

Mike walked across the room and picked up her rumpled blouse. He held out his hand to help her stand up. She placed her hand in his and stood.

"I'm sorry," he said, holding out the blouse.

Holly quickly put on the blouse. "You've got nothing to be sorry for."

"My timing could have been better . . . for both our sakes. Come to the show with me. I don't want to be far from you tonight."

They arrived at the studio thirty minutes before showtime. He hadn't completely relaxed when he'd arrived, so he wore the oversized jacket to his suit. Holly was quiet on the ride down. It had taken some convincing to get her to come tonight, but he couldn't leave her in his house alone. He didn't want her to get cold feet and go home.

He watched her study the video collection in his office and remembered her face when he'd stroked her breasts. He remembered the way she'd arched her back and held his hands over them. Feeling his manhood stir, he dragged his thoughts away from her and attempted to concentrate on the list of questions for tonight's guests. When the time came to go out on stage, he was glad that he wore the suit with loose, baggy pants and a large jacket. The show seemed to drag on. Although he knew that the show lasted the same amount of time, he was ready for the guests to leave. The only time that he forgot to be anxious to leave was when the singer walked to Holly, who was standing off to the side of the stage, and led her out on the stage as he sang his last song, which was a love song.

It was at that moment that Mike realized that he loved her. Lightning didn't flash across the sky and thunder didn't roll. He just felt a quiet assurance that this was the woman he wanted to marry. He watched as she blushed under the attention of the singer. When the song finished and the singer kissed her hand, Holly looked over at him, ignoring the man whom women from all over the world would do just about anything to get close to. But it was him she wanted. Mike could still detect traces of desire in her eyes when they met his, the same desire that she'd displayed earlier in his bedroom.

Finally, the show was over and the audience started filing out of the studio. Mike ran through post-production with the speed of a madman. Several times people asked him what was his hurry. For the first time, he left the studio before post-production was complete. Members of his staff stared after him when he and Holly left the studio and they were the cause of gossip that evening. But Mike only had making love to Holly on his mind. Quickly, he drove from the studio to his house. He held her hand as they walked to the bedroom without saying a word. The passion that was banked this evening burst into flames as they entered his room. The soft light from the lamps on the two night-stands created an intimate glow in the room.

Mike picked her up and gently laid her on his bed. He knew that nothing was going to stop them from making love tonight. And it would be love on his part. He removed her shoes and tossed them on the floor. He stood beside the bed and looked at her. Then he took off his jacket and unbuttoned his shirt and tossed them on the floor next to her shoes.

"You have on too many clothes." He sat down on the edge of the bed. Then reached across to gently unbutton her shirt. Her bra was removed, along with her shirt. Hungrily his mouth closed over her nipple, and he caressed the other with his hand.

Desire, hot and powerful, surged though her body to the very depths of her. She could feel the urgency in him as she caressed and held his head to her chest. "Michael, oh, Mike."

He felt a wave of satisfaction as she arched her back, thrusting her breasts forward. He turned and suckled her. Then he kissed his way across to the middle of her chest. He spread leisurely kisses down her stomach and felt a thrill when she moaned.

"Do you like that, sweet?" He spaced each word with a kiss. "Or do you like this?" He unbuckled and unzipped her red pants. Spreading the fabric, he exposed her belly and the white lace panties that matched her bra. He bent his head and traced the outline of her navel before touching the nub of her navel with his tongue, mimicking the caress she'd given him just hours ago.

He felt the bite of her nails into his shoulders.

He heard her incoherent moans. "I've wanted to do this all day." Rising to his knees, he slowly slid her pants down and off. He sucked in his breath at the sight of her. A sharp wave of desire shot directly to his already heavy manhood.

She was on fire. The feelings that overcame her were like nothing she'd ever experienced before. She couldn't get enough of his touch. She sat up in bed. She reached for his belt buckle, then unzipped his pants. The familiar white briefs appeared. She slipped her fingers just beneath the elastic waistband. He held his breath as she pulled his pants and briefs down to his knees.

Holly forgot to be shy when she saw him nude for the first time. He was magnificent. Thick, wide shoulders tapered down to slim, firm hips. A thick thatch of black hair covered the base of his hard, broad manhood. His long, powerful thighs were covered with thin, fine black hair. He looked like everything that a lover should be . . . hard, long, and ready.

Mike kicked off his pants, then leaned her back against the pillows on the bed, turning her on her side to face him. They shared a single pillow. He brushed the back of his fingers along her shoulder and down her arm and he laced his fingers through hers. He brought her hand to his chest and held it there.

"Touch me, Holly."

His heart pounded beneath her hand. Hesitantly at first, she caressed his chest, but she became bolder. She moved closer to him and kissed his lips gently, then, with more force, increased her passion.

Her hot, open-mouth kisses were returned in spades. Her hand traveled from his chest and down his stomach before sliding through the thick patch of hair to the very tip of his manhood. With the tips of her fingers, she drew lazy circles around the tip of him. She stroked the length of him.

"Yes, Holly, yes!" He rocked his hips against her tender caress. His hand tightened against her waist before cupping her buttocks. He ran his hand down her thigh to her knee. He groaned when she began the milking strokes up and down his manhood. The pleasure that she gave him almost undid him. He reached between them and took her hand.

"I can't take much more of that." He moved her hands to his chest and she instantly began stroking, touching, and caressing him. He held her hands firmly against him, curbing her movement until she was still. He placed her arms at her sides and reached across the bed to his nightstand. He quickly put on a condom before returning his full attention to her.

Mike stroked her knee, gently guiding her until they lay on their sides facing each other. He slid closer to her and slid his thigh between her legs. He moved his hands to the soft curly hair that covered her, stroking until he found the small nub hidden within her folds. Tears streamed down her cheeks when he brushed the pad of his thumb across it. A fire seemed to consume her body. Her hips bucked against his hand.

"I can't take it. I can't take it," she chanted, and nearly screamed when he slipped his finger inside her.

"You're so beautiful." He marveled at her response. She was wet and ready for him. He moved her thigh around his waist. "Open your eyes, sweet. Look at me."

She opened her brown eyes and looked into his. Slowly, ever so slowly, he entered her. Her body stretched to accommodate him. He filled her. He pulled out slightly, then slid back into her. Her fingers bit into his shoulders. He rocked his hips against her in a slow, steady pace. Her body clinched around him.

"Oh, you feel so good. So good." He rocked faster, deeper, against her.

Holly felt a tension building within her. It was like a small spot on the horizon, but as he stroked her body, the tension became larger, stronger . . . until she felt it overwhelm her in its power. She moved her hips achingly against his, trying to relieve that strange, pulsating tension.

"Let go, baby." Mike moved faster against her. Holly wrapped her arms around him, pulling him closer to her. Then an explosion of pleasure rippled through her. The tension which had been building inside her snapped. She thrust her hips against him, arching her back.

Mike felt her body contract around him and he watched her as she found pleasure. Her head thrust back and her eyes closed. She looked as if she were in exquisite pain or in the most wonderful pleasure.

He waited until she received her pleasure before allowing himself to be overcome by the pleasure of his release.

Later that evening, Holly groaned sleepily when

he eased gently out of her and walked to his bath-room.

When Mike came back into the room, he turned off the lamps, throwing the room into darkness. He slid into bed and wrapped her in his arms.

Holly dreamed that she had fallen asleep on the beach with the warm sand beneath her and the bright sun shining down on her. She snuggled deeper in the sand. Then, suddenly, the sand moved, wrapping itself around her waist.

Holly came out of her dream and squinted her eyes against the bright sun shining through the windows in Mike's bedroom. She knew instantly where she was, and it wasn't the beach. She looked down at the "sand," which was Mike's arm wrapped possessively around her waist, and just as in her dream, the sun was shining down upon her.

She lifted her head to look at the alarm clock on the nightstand and dropped her head back on the pillow. It was ten o'clock. Pam was probably ready to call the police by now when she didn't show up at the office. She could imagine what she did when she'd called Holly's house and gotten no answer.

Holly carefully tried to move Mike's arm without waking him. Instead of releasing, her like she'd planned, his arm tightened around her, drawing her closer to him. After several failed attempts to move his arm, she realized that she wouldn't get out of that bed without waking him. She turned in his embrace and looked at him.

His expression was one of total peace. His long,

thick lashes rested on his cheeks. She felt a well of tenderness as she looked at him. A faint stubble covered his jaw, and his lips were slightly parted as he slept.

"Mike," she said softly, and caressed his cheek. Slowly he opened his eyes and looked at her. Then he pulled her closer in his embrace.

"Tell me that this isn't a dream and you are here with me." His voice was husky with sleep.

"It's not a dream."

"Good. Then I can make love to you again."

Holly felt the desire all the way down to her toes. What was it about this man, that she couldn't get enough of him? "Before you do, I need to call the office and tell them not to expect me."

"Okay," he said, without moving.

"Mike, you need to let me go so I can reach the phone."

Reluctantly he moved his arm. Holly sat up and reached for the phone. When she dialed the office, Robyn connected her directly with Pam.

"Hi, Pam."

"Where the hell are you?"

"Good morning to you, too." Holly laughed at the snap in Pam's voice. "I'm sorry I didn't call earlier, but I'm not going to be in today."

There was silence on the other end of the line for a moment. "You're not coming in the office and you sound like you just woke up. Hmmmm. Sounds like you've been having yourself a good old time."

Mike reached across the bed and began to caress her thighs.

"I've got to go now, Pam."

"You might want to call your brother. He was worried when you didn't answer the phone last night and this morning."

"I'll call him later," Holly said in a husky voice.

"Just one other thing, Holly." Pam paused, then yelled into the phone, "Hi, Mike!"

Mike laughed, and said, "Hi, Pam. Holly's got to go now."

" 'Bye Pam." Holly hung up the phone and put it on the nightstand. Mike pulled her down in the bed.

"You look a little tired, sweet." He caressed her face with the back of his fingers. "Why don't you just lie down and rest for a while?" He brushed his lips over hers. Passion sprung up between them and it was lunchtime before they made it out of bed.

"It doesn't feel right, eating pancakes at one o'clock in the afternoon," Holly said, as she cut the fluffy brown cakes covered with real maple syrup.

"Somewhere in the world it's time to eat breakfast. Just pretend that you're there."

Holly glared at him. "Yeah, right."

"Some people have no imagination, no vision . . ."

"Some people have a strong sense of reality," she interrupted.

"Just eat, woman." He gave her a mock frown before he reached across the table and squeezed her hand.

Several times today, he'd almost told her that he loved her. But he knew that she wasn't ready to hear that now. She probably wouldn't believe he really loved her. He was determined to prove his love for her. He would make her forget about moving to Seattle, and together they would build a life together.

He looked at her from across the table. She had brushed her hair back off her face, leaving it loose. Her face was free of makeup, but beautiful nonetheless. Her face was the one he wanted to see across his table for the rest of his life.

"I've got to go home and change," she said, when they'd finished their breakfast. She stood and gathered the dishes to take in the kitchen.

"Okay. I've got to make a call. It shouldn't take long," he said, and followed her to the kitchen.

Henry looked up from the chicken that he was deboning. He didn't look happy to see them. Holly felt as if she had entered his personal space and nearly backed out of the door until she bumped into Mike.

"Holly?" Mike gently nudged her in the back.

She smiled weakly at the giant of a man. "Good afternoon."

Henry nodded at her and continued to cut the chicken.

"Hi, Henry," Mike said, and walked to the dishwasher. They loaded the dishwasher and Holly jumped when Henry started to chop up the chicken with a cleaver.

Ten

They never made it to Holly's house; they never even made it out of Mike's front door. The drawstring shorts that Mike gave her to wear hung loosely on her hips and the T-shirt was almost as long as the shorts. The way she was dressed was the last thing on her mind.

Holly looked down at the blackened blobs on the plate. "Are you sure you don't want the Chicken Kiev that Henry made?"

"No, I want a hamburger."

"Mike, I think we should give cooking a rest now."

"Let me try it just one more time," he said, standing in front of the stove, molding another beef patty in his hand. He had incinerated four hamburger patties within thirty minutes. The windows in the breakfast area of the kitchen were open. The ceiling fan and the fan above the stove made a valiant attempt to blow the smoke out of the room.

"You might try scrubbing the pan, instead of getting a new one." Holly looked at the stack of dishes in the sink.

"Why? I've got two more pans." Mike reached

under the cabinet for a clean pan with one hand, holding the hamburger with the other.

"You can leave those dirty dishes for Henry if you want to, but I don't think he'll appreciate it." She leaned against the counter and watched the muscles in his back ripple against the cotton T-shirt.

He placed the pan on the stove. "A dishwasher works wonders. Tell me again: how do you know if it's done?" Mike put the newly formed patty on a plate beside the stove and looked at her with a puzzled expression.

Holly sighed. How could a man so dedicated and focused at work be such a total disaster in the kitchen? The least little thing could distract him. A telephone call, the instructions on the back of carton of macaroni and cheese, and the stack of letters on the kitchen counter were the causes of his distraction.

"You have to concentrate on cooking, Mike. Concentrate on cooking. That's all— nothing else. No phone calls, no reading the mail, nothing!"

"Okay."

"Now, turn on the stove." She watched him turn the knob until the flame was at its highest setting. "You don't want the hamburger to burn, so make the flame about half that height, then put the hamburger in the frying pan . . ."

An hour later, Mike and Holly sat at his dinette table. Their meal consisted of hamburger and fries from a popular fast-food restaurant. The late-afternoon sun cast a brilliant glow in his kitchen. The smoky, acid-like smell still lingered in the room.

"Hmmm. This burger is great. Not a charred,

burned, or seared spot on it." Holly bit into her hamburger and glanced at Mike with amusement.

"That's so low-down." Mike unwrapped his hamburger.

"I'd really be low-down to mention that some young kid can make not one but two hamburgers and not have a burnt spot on either burger. And that same kid still had time to ask for your autograph."

"Hey! The last hamburger wasn't bad," he said, before taking a bite of his own hamburger.

"Okay, your last try wasn't bad, if you like them burnt on the outside and raw on the inside. How in the world did you survive before you could afford your own chef?"

"I ate out mostly, but when I stayed home, I ate frozen dinners."

"Yuk! That stuff tastes like Styrofoam. I'd rather not eat at all."

"They aren't so bad, once you convince yourself that they aren't supposed to taste like the food your mother made." Mike gave her a mocking glare, then said in a snobbish tone of voice, "Your affluent upbringing is showing."

"My affluent upbringing has nothing to do with tasteless frozen dinners. Didn't you pick up any cooking tips from your mother when you were growing up?"

"Nope. Dinner was done by the time I got home from school. I went to private school about fifty miles away from home after the second grade."

"You went to a private school in the second grade?" Holly waved a French fry at him in a way that reminded him of his mother shaking her finger at him when he'd done something wrong. Motherly thoughts were the last thing on his mind. He watched her take a bite of the french fry, then lick ketchup from her fingers.

"And you talk about my affluent upbringing," she said. "So you and your brothers didn't get to know the kids in the neighborhood."

"My brothers knew them because they went to the local school. I was the only one who didn't go."

"Why were you the only one who didn't go to local school?" she asked curiously.

Mike slowly dipped a french fry into the pool of ketchup. "In the first grade, they gave us an intelligence test." He paused, then said in a slightly embarrassed tone, "I scored high on the test."

Her eyes grew wide with surprise. "You mean, you were a boy genius?"

"Yeah, I was a real genius," he said sheepishly.

"What was that like?"

"I took a lot of tests in the first couple of years." Annoyance flashed across his face. "Then there was that long, boring bus ride to school everyday."

"It must have been hard to be separated from your brothers like that." Her eyes were filled with sympathy.

"It wasn't so bad. My parents made sure that I kept my feet on the ground and my brothers in line. The teasing never got too far out of line. Mom and Dad wanted me to have a regular childhood, regardless."

"What about the other kids in the neighborhood? Did they give you a hard time?"

Mike smiled, then said, "No. I wasn't your typical gifted child. I could play ball or get into fights like the rest of the kids. After a while, my going to a different school didn't make me any different."

"But didn't you ever want to go the same school with your brothers and your friends?"

"I did once. In the twelfth grade, I decided that I was tired of the accelerated class and bugged my parents until they let me go to the local high school. The only problem was, I was younger than everybody in the class, and my older brother was in the same class. I didn't know how to deal with people trying to cheat off of me because nobody thought about cheating at the other school. My brother was harassed because his little brother was smarter than he was. It was a bad decision all the way around. I lasted for about three weeks, then went back to the school were I was before."

"Oh, you poor baby." Holly could imagine him as a teenager trying to fit into a world so different than what he was accustomed to.

Mike laughed. "Don't feel sorry for me. I milked my intelligence for all it was worth while I was there. I thought that I was showing them that I belonged when all I was doing was making my classmates feel stupid. Thirteen-year-old boys aren't known for their common sense, and I didn't have any at the time."

Mike laughed about the incident, but she heard the trace of hurt and confusion in his voice. She knew what it was like to want to fit in, to be accepted and get rejected.

"That's enough about me. What were you like at thirteen?"

"Oh, please. I don't want to remember that year."

"Why?"

"That was the year that Daddy became mayor of Atlanta. It was a pretty awful time for me, following daddy around the different parts of the city . . . smiling all the time, trying to look happy to be there, when all I wanted to do was go home." Holly shuttered. "And the people. People were every-where. I felt claustrophobic."

"But that didn't last too long."

"Yes, it did. There was a run-off and we had to start campaigning all over again. The worst were the reporters. Since Daddy was the first black mayor of a large city, the election got national attention and national press."

"What was so bad about it?"

"It's hard to pick just one thing. Maybe being in the spotlight with everyone watching. I felt like everyone was waiting for me to make a mistake. It seemed like everything I did wrong was somewhere in the paper or on the news. It would have been different if the whole family was picked on, but no one else in the family got the razzing that I did. If I had a run in my stocking, there would be a picture of me with the run showing."

"Maybe it just seemed like they were singling you out. If the same things happened today, you might not see the press as isolating you. You're older and better able to cope with the bad press than you were at thirteen."

"I don't know if I cope with the press any better than I did at thirteen."

"Yes, you do. I don't think that anyone else could have handled the press better than you did when Trey got married. As a matter of fact, I think you outmaneuvered Trey when you told the reporter that you were hurt that a friend would treat you the way he did. Trey and his publicist had to forget about making his sudden marriage the love story of the century after your quote."

Holly smiled. "He did seem mad when he was asked to respond to what I'd said. His new wife wasn't happy about the question, either."

Mike studied her face for a moment, then nodded, as if he'd come to a decision. "Come on." He rose from the table. "There's something I want to show you."

They walked downstairs to the lower level, where the gym and the entertainment room were located. Mike opened the double doors to the entertainment room, then stood in the doorway, blocking her entrance. "Before I show you this, you've got to promise you won't talk about this to anybody else."

Puzzled at the earnest expression on his face, Holly agreed.

"Make yourself comfortable on the sofa. This could take a while."

She sat on the overstuffed sofa and watched as he pressed buttons on a wall panel. The blinds covering the windows closed and the lights dimmed until Holly could barely see Mike on the other side of the room. Mike walked toward her. She heard the sound of a motor, then realized he had lowered a huge video screen. He sat down beside her, then lifted his arm as if to use a remote control device. Mike's face appeared on the screen. "Hello, I'm here to set the record straight. I did not sleep with the following women: Madonna, Whitney Houston, Cher, Robin Givens, Tracey Alexander, or Donna Ross. I don't have any children, and I am not gay. That's all I have to say." The screen was black for a moment, then there were video clips of Mike appearing on various television shows. They were a series of Mike's mistakes on film.

"Is that you?" Holly asked with disbelief, as a shot of a much younger Mike appeared on screen. He was dressed in a shirt and tie and appeared to be reporting live on a human interest segment for a local television station. The more Mike spoke, the less the guest spoke, until Mike was the only one talking. Holly was still laughing an hour later when the film ended.

"You can stop laughing now," Mike said, using the remote control to open the blinds.

"I can't believe you did all that. How can you get in front of a camera every night, knowing that you could totally screw up?"

Mike turned to her, his expression serious and somber. "Everybody makes mistakes. You just learn from your mistakes, and hopefully, you won't make the same ones again. If I didn't go out there every night, I would be cheating myself. I can't let fear stop me from doing what I love."

Holly tensed at his words. She'd had a wonderful time up until now. Was she letting fear drive her away from her business? She loved running Security

Force; owning Tamp Security wouldn't be the same. Tamp Security wasn't her creation.

Mike continued, "The one thing I've learned is that you can't run away from your problems. No matter where you go in this world, usually, your problems follow you."

Holly felt uneasy. Mike's words touched the very thing she had feared the most: that she'd leave Atlanta and she still wouldn't have a private life. No, she wouldn't let fear or anything else stop her from leaving. If Mike tried to talk her out of leaving Atlanta, they, would argue, and she didn't want to fight, but she would.

"Hey." Mike waved his hand in front her face. "Are you still with me? I brought two black cowboy movies. Do you want to see them?"

While Mike loaded the tapes into the VCR, Holly breath a sigh of relief. He hadn't pushed her, but she knew that it was just a matter of time before they'd have to discuss her move to Seattle and their time together would be close to an end.

She was dangerously close to falling in love with Michael Williams, Holly thought, as she prepared for bed that evening. Mike had aroused feelings that Trey had never been able to evoke in her when they were engaged. Those feelings scared her. The tenderness, the warmth, the undeniable passion bloomed when she was with him. She turned back the comforter on her bed and lay down on the cool, white cotton sheets. *It's just physical*, she muttered, closing her eyes in an attempt to fall asleep, determined to ignore the doubt in her heart.

Her eyes opened when her telephone rang a moment later. She looked at her clock before answering.

"Hello," she said softly.

"Where have you been, Holly?" Robert, Jr., snapped. "I've been trying to get in touch with you since last night!"

Holly laid her head on her pillow and closed her eyes. She'd been so involved with Mike that she'd forgotten to return his call.

"I'm sorry, Robert. I forgot to call you back."

"We were worried about you." His irritation with her was apparent in his tone.

"We?" she asked, dreading his answer.

"Dad, Grandma, and I were planning to invite you out for dinner tonight. I called yesterday to see if you could come, but obviously you weren't at home."

"No. I wasn't." A tense silence stretched between them.

Robert broke the silence. "Where were you last night?"

"You're on shaky ground, little brother." A steel-like quality entered her tone.

"Is everything okay, Holly?" he asked with concern.

"Everything's fine," she said softly. "I'm sorry that I missed dinner with ya'll."

"Yeah, me, too. Goodnight, Holly."

"Goodnight."

Robert, Jr., hung up the telephone and sat on

the edge of the bed. He was worried about her. First, she'd planned to move to Seattle and hadn't informed the family. Now, she was staying out all night. That wasn't like her at all. He'd learned from Pam this afternoon that Holly had gone out with Michael Williams last night. He had nothing against Mike Williams; he didn't know the man. Robert, Jr., grimaced. He hadn't known Trey, either, when he'd introduced him to Holly. He left his room and walked downstairs to his father's home office. It was time he and Dad had a talk.

Mike had been summoned. There was no other way to describe the tone Holly's grandmother had used when "inviting" him to lunch the following day. Apparently, Holly and her grandmother had the same taste in restaurants. They'd both suggested the Private Room. He was informed by the waiter that Mrs. Nola Aimes was already at a table. Mike checked his watch. He was five minutes early. He followed the waiter to their table. Mike was surprised to see not only Holly's grandmother, but her father as well.

"Mrs. Aimes, Senator."

"Call me Nola, young man," she said, as the two men shook hands.

"I'm glad we finally got a chance to talk," Holly's father said. "Call me Robert. 'Senator' sounds too pompous."

"Well, now that we've gotten all the niceties settled." She leveled him with a piercing look.

"Mama," Holly's father said with a warning tone.

Nola ignored her son. "What are your intentions toward my granddaughter?"

"What happened to subtlety, Mama?"

"Robert, I'm seventy-seven years old. I might not see tomorrow. I don't have time for subtlety."

Mike had to struggle not to smile. This sounded like an ongoing argument between the two, he thought.

"Hush, son. This young man hasn't answered my question." She looked at Mike with expectation.

"There you are." Jean Aimes rushed ahead of the waiter, her son trailing behind.

"Can't do a thing in this town without the whole world knowing about it," Nola muttered, then glared at her son. "How did they know about this meeting?"

"There are no secrets in my house, Mama."

"Next time, come to *my* house," Nola said impatiently. "Hurry and sit down. Mike was just about to answer my question."

"What was the question?" Jean asked, as she and Robert, Jr., settled in empty chairs.

"Nola wanted to know what were my intentions toward Holly." The attention of all focused on him. He carefully chose his words before speaking. "I love Holly and I plan to be in her life for as long as she'll have me."

Nola beamed at him. "So when are you going to marry her?"

"Mother!"

"Grandma!"

"I want to know when the boy is going to marry her." She glared at her family. "Now, hush."

Mike smiled at her. "When Holly and I decide to get married, you'll be the first to know, Nola." At first, Mike was taken aback by his words, but a sense of fulfillment replaced his surprise. It was as if his heart had known and accepted his love for her before he had ever spoken the words to himself or to Holly.

"What's this I hear about your interview with Trey Christian?" Robert, Jr., leaned forward in his chair. "Holly's had enough bad press. She doesn't deserve any more."

"The interview I have planned for him will be on his upcoming movie. I'd ask you the same questions if you were on my show."

"Trey is a son-of-a . . ."

"Junior, watch your mouth."

"Sorry." He gave his grandmother a sheepish grin before turning to Mike. The grin melted and his expression was serious. "Trey doesn't care for anybody but Trey. He's used his past relationship with Holly as a publicity stunt more than once. Holly is the one who ends up being hurt. I don't want that to happen on your show."

"Don't worry. I'll make sure he sticks to answering my questions. If he doesn't, he'll be the one who looks like a fool."

"I like your style, young man," Nola said.

With that statement, the interrogation by the Aimes family was over for Mike. Or so he thought. After lunch, the rest of the family left the restaurant.

Holly's father hung behind. "Before you leave, Mike, I'd like a word with you."

"Sure." Mike leaned back in his chair, waiting for the older man to speak.

"My daughter has been through a lot this past year. Unfortunately, I wasn't able . . . no, I didn't take the time to thoroughly investigate Trey before Holly was hurt. I won't make that same mistake again."

"Robert . . ."

The senator held up his hand. "Let me finish. Holly means the world to me. I know sometimes she's thought that I've forgotten about her and that I love Sandra and Robert, Jr., more than I love her. That's not true. So if you have any doubts about your feelings toward her, end the relationship now. Because if you hurt her," he put his forearm on the table and leaned forward, and the pleasant politician expression was replaced by a stern 'I mean business' expression, "I'll make you wish you'd never seen the light of day."

"I love Holly. I have no doubt about it."

"Good. That's what I wanted to hear." He looked at his watch and stood. "I've got a meeting. It's been nice talking with you, Mike." He held out his hand.

"Same here." They shook hands and Mike watched as the senator left. If that was his idea of a "talk," Mike thought, he'd hate to be around when he threatened somebody.

"Will that be all, sir?" the waiter asked.

Mike reached for his wallet and pulled out a credit card, "Yes, that's it."

"The bill is taken care of, sir. Have a nice afternoon."

As Mike drove to his office, he wondered if Holly

realized how much her family loved her. But as much as her family loved her, he knew that Holly felt like an outsider. He'd make sure that she never had a doubt that he loved her. All he had to do was to convince her not to move to Seattle. He didn't have much time to convince her, but convince her he would.

He had the support of her family and her best friend. A wicked smile crossed his face. He wondered how she'd react when she learned about today's lunch meeting. He picked up his car phone and began to dial her number.

Eleven

"He was safe! He was safe!" Mike jumped to his feet and shouted along with the rest of the Atlanta Braves fans in the stadium.

Holly smiled as she listened to insults and statements of disbelief Mike aimed at the umpire. She hadn't seen that type of hand movement and finger gesturing since her last trip to New York City. He seemed impervious to the ninety-four-degree heat and nearly one-hundred-percent humidity. He and the baseball player who was called out argued passionately against the call. "Don't you think you're being hard on the man?" she asked, when he finally sat in his seat.

"Hard?" he said, clutching the half-empty bag of peanuts. "The man is obviously blind and he doesn't know a thing about baseball."

"That must be why they hired him as the umpire," she said, as she tugged on the brim of the Braves cap Mike had bought for her at the start of the game.

Mike looked at her. His brown eyes narrowed. She saw a flicker of annoyance in his eyes, then his expression changed to one of amusement. "Smart aleck," he said, as he placed his arm along the back of her seat. He gently squeezed her shoulder before returning his attention to the baseball field.

The smell of greasy hot dogs and popcorn permeated in the box seats. The two teams played a close game, but in the seventh inning, the Braves were losing by a score of five to three. The hot sun beat down on her bare legs. She enjoyed watching Mike almost as much as she enjoyed the baseball game. He was an intense fan, jumping to his feet when the Braves scored and moaning in grief when things weren't going their way.

She was glad that she'd changed her mind at the last minute and agreed to go with him. They'd both tiptoed around the subject of her move to Seattle. It was as if they'd called a nonverbal truce, Holly thought. In a few days, the Milton Group would award the bid. She was confident that her company would win and the delicate truce between them would end. "I'm not going to think about that now," Holly said to herself, and concentrated on the action unfolding on the playing field.

She didn't know what distracted her from the game. Later, when she had time to think about the events, she would wonder whether it was the sound of the tub of Coke falling onto the seats beside her or the audible intake of breath that distracted her. At any rate, the events that occurred were Holly's worst nightmare.

The group of teenagers seated to the right of their box made as much noise as Mike did. During the seventh inning stretch, they stood listening to the piped-in music over the speaker system. Mike took off his baseball cap and sunglasses and smiled at her.

"Are you having a good time?" he asked.

"I'm having more fun watching you watch the game." Holly took his hand in hers. "I never knew you could convey so many thoughts with the flip of a hand."

His expression was sheepish. "I tend to get carried away."

"I would never have guessed." As the sound of the last note of a popular tune ended, Holly heard the thump. When she turned toward the sound, she saw a teenaged girl. The tub of Coke rolled like a tidal wave down the bleachers. The fans sitting in the seats below made a mad dash to avoid the wave of soft drink. But the teenager didn't hear their sounds of surprise. Her eyes were focused on Mike.

Holly heard the girl's quick gasp of breath. She shouted, "Oh, my God!" She ran toward the box seats, shouting "It's him! It's Mike Williams. Oh, God. Oh, God!" The girl climbed over the gate separating their box seat from the rest of the seats. In her excitement, the girl would have knocked Holly over if Mike hadn't pulled Holly into his arms.

"Is it you? Are you really Mike Williams?"

Mike looked at the girl, then met Holly's gaze. His expression was apologetic. He looked at the excited fan and smiled. "Yes, I'm Mike Williams."

The scream she let loose caught the attention of the fans around them. "I watch your show every night," she gasped, and turned to her friends at the end of the row. "Christy! Michelle! It's Mike Williams!"

It was as if the floodgates had been opened, Holly thought, as she sat in Mike's seat. There wasn't enough room to get into her seat. Fans surrounded them. Mike signed his autographs on everything from a napkin to the back of a T-shirt a fan was wearing. Holly watched as Mike handled the crowd with grace. Gone was the man having fun at a baseball game. In his place was Mike Williams the talk-show host.

Holly gasped with pain as another fan tried to get closer to Mike. She tried to make herself as small as possible, but no matter how many times she shifted positions, someone humped her shoulder as they reached over her or stepped on her foot as they tried to walk around her.

"Mr. Williams." Holly recognized the man as a sports reporter on a local television channel. Standing behind the reporter was a cameraman with a minicam in position. "How about a few words about the game?" he asked, holding out a microphone.

Holly barely heard Mike's response. If she could have left without the reporter seeing her, she would have. She hoped that the crowd would be large enough to hide her from the reporter.

"What do you think about the game, Ms. Aimes?" Holly froze for a split second. "I think that this is a tough game for the Braves, and I hope they win." She smiled halfheartedly and looked at the reporter. She nearly sighed in relief as the reporter began to wrap up the interview.

"Hey, I got a question." The loud, raspy voice

pierced the noisy buzz of the crowd. Dressed in rumpled tan pants and a navy golf shirt that barely covered the large beer belly, Stan Winfield, of *The Inquiry,* stood with tape recorder in hand. *The Inquiry* was the type of newspaper that printed stories whether they were true or not true. No one was immune to their brand of journalism. Holly's and Trey's pictures had appeared on their front pages for weeks after their broken engagement. Stan Winfield smiled at Holly. She saw the cameraman turn with the minicam still recording the scene. She shivered despite the heat when she saw the gleam in Stan's eyes. "Think you'll be able to keep this one, Miss Aimes?"

Mike turned down the street to her home. The only sound in the car came from the radio. Mike had tried to talk to Holly, but her response had been apathetic at best. Cars and vans were parked on both sides of her street. Photographers and reporters milled around her front door.

"What is this?" Mike asked in disgust.

Holly felt cold dread fill her body. Not again, she thought. She was glad that his car had tinted windows. "Please drive by like you're going somewhere else."

Holly glanced briefly at the reporters standing in her yard before turning her gaze to her tightly clenched hands in her lap. The scene brought back memories of the weeks after her botched engagement: the constant questions, the lack of privacy . . .

This is why I should have never gotten involved with Mike . . .

"Oh, hell," Mike muttered. "One of them spotted us." Holly turned and looked out the back window. Several people were running to their cars, ready to give chase. Mike gunned the engine and raced through her neighborhood.

"Do you know any other exits out of here?" Mike asked.

Holly give him directions and they headed out of the subdivision. For a few tense moments the trail of cars followed them, but he lost them on a one-way street.

Mike pulled into a service station and turned to her. "Why don't you call someone to get you some clothes?"

"No, just drop me off at the office and I'll drive my car home."

"You don't want to go back to that madhouse." He stared at her, puzzled. "I'm not going to let you go there and face them alone."

"I've faced them alone before, and you won't always be there for me."

He couldn't believe that she'd said that to him. "I'm here for you now . . . so take advantage of it."

"It'll only make it worse if I don't appear at home. I might as well get it over with." Looking at his car phone, she asked, "Can I use your phone?"

He agreed. Holly dialed the office. "Hi, Robyn. Is Pam there?"

"Yes, she's here. Holly, you're not coming back in today, are you?"

"No. Why?"

"We had a swarm of reporter here about thirty minutes ago. Some of them are still outside. They were looking for you."

"Great."

"I'm sorry. Let me transfer you to Pam."

"Hey, Holly," Pam said. "Whatever you do, don't come here. The reporters are swarming like bees."

"Where do you want to go, home or work?" he asked, when she'd ended her conversation with Pam.

"Neither. I just wish they'd leave me alone." Holly leaned her head back against her seat.

"You're going to have to face them sometime. It's either now or later," he continued, when she didn't respond. "The best thing to do is to just get it over with."

"The best thing would have been never to let this thing happen in the first place," she said sadly.

"What could you have done to avoid it?" he said softly. "You didn't know Stan Winfield would be at the Braves game."

No, she didn't know Stan Winfield would be at the game, but she should have known that someone like him would show up sooner or later. It was her relationship with Mike that had cause the renewed media attention. She would have to either end their relationship now or continue to see Mike until she moved to Seattle. Either solution would end in pain on her part.

As she looked at his concerned expression, she

realized that she had done what she was afraid she would do and that was to fall in love with Mike.

There. She'd admitted it. She was in love with him. She had denied her feelings last night, determined to pretend that she'd only found him sexually attractive. But now, sitting here in the parking lot of a self-service gas station, she could tell herself that she was in love.

Mike drove Holly home and no amount of arguing on her part would change his mind. Silence filled the car as they drove through her neighborhood. There weren't as many cars parked along the street, but the reporters were there nonetheless.

Mike drove into her driveway and parked the car. The reporters gathered around, camera lenses pointing and poised to take their pictures. Mike held her hand for a brief second, then opened his door.

"What brings you guys here?" he said, as if he were talking to friends.

"Could you tell us when you and Ms. Aimes started your relationship?"

"Were you seeing her while she was engaged?"

"How about a picture of the both of you together, Mike?"

"Neither of us has any comment, guys." Mike walked around his car, bumping microphones out of the way until he reached the passenger side. He opened the door for her.

The whir of camera motors increased as he helped her out of the car.

"Ms. Aimes, when did you get over your feelings for Trey Christian?"

"Have you and Mr. Williams been dating long?"

Holly hated this, and Mike was playing along with them. He was actually smiling as if he were enjoying this circus. He was acting like Trey . . . lapping up the attention with no regard for her feelings.

They made their way to her front door. Her hands shook as she dug in her purse for the key.

"We've going to have to ask you to leave now," Mike said, as Holly opened the door. With a firm snap, he shut the door, ignoring the rapid fire of questions.

Mike locked the door. She went to the control panel of her alarm system and disengaged it. Mike walked to her. "See? That wasn't so hard now, was it?"

Holly turned to him, her shoulders rigid with anger. "Why did you talk to them? If you wanted some free publicity, why didn't you just wait until I was inside?"

His hands rested on her shoulders and he frowned in confusion. "What are you talking about?"

"You know I wanted to avoid them." Holly stepped away from him. "But you were just talking with them like this was some Hollywood premiere. I don't like it. I didn't like it when Trey did it, and I don't like it now."

"I was trying to make it easy for you. I was trying to put as much attention on me as I could so that they would lighten up on you." Mike's fingers tightened on her shoulders. "Don't you ever accuse me of using you for publicity. My name is Mike, not Trey." He released her arms and walked across to the other side of the living room and sighed. "Look, why don't I come back after the show? We both need time to calm down," he said.

He was sure that it was just her emotions talking now. Once she thought about it, she had to know that he was nothing like Trey Christian. He'd wanted to share the day with her, but he could see how the press had upset her. "I'll see you after the show."

She thought about the reporters and the captions they would put under the pictures of him coming to her house after midnight. "No. Don't come tonight. It will just fuel the talk."

"Holly, they're going to talk about us in the newspapers and magazines and on television no matter *what* we do. We're the item of the week now. Soon, they'll get wind of somebody else. Then they'll start following them. That's the way they work. It's their job. You can't let what they say about us govern how you live your life."

"Please, Mike. I just don't want to deal with them right now." Holly turned away from him.

He could feel her tension from across the room. He sighed. "All right, Holly. I'll call you tonight." He walked to the front door. He turned to look back at her before opening the door and walking out.

Later that evening, Holly lay on her sofa in the den, listening as the national news ended and *Inside Entertainment,* a nightly program dedicated to Hollywood entertainment news, began. She sat up on the sofa when the announcer said her name.

"Could it be love for the second time? Michael

Williams and Holly Aimes, who you'll remember as
Trey Christian's former fiancée, were seen together
several times in Atlanta. Mike Williams, who has
been nominated again for an Emmy, has been
linked with cover girl Sally and actress Erica Long.
This is the first time he's been seen with someone
outside the entertainment industry. *IE* was able to
obtain footage of the couple arriving at Ms. Aimes's
home outside of Atlanta." The television picture
changed to show her and Mike walking to her
house. There was a blurb of Mike telling the reporters that they had no comment. The announcer
continued, "On his Thursday night show, Trey
Christian will be his guest. It should be interesting
to see what questions he has for the actor.

"Trey Christian's engagement to the daughter of
Governor Bob Aimes of Georgia was the object of
massive media attention. Holly Aimes's life seemed
like a fairy tale, a handsome prince marrying the
woman hailed as the 'ugly duckling' in the family.
But her fairy tale became a nightmare when her
fiancé married supermodel Marla Johnson one
week after announcing their engagement. We'll
have reaction to Thursday night's show on *Inside
Entertainment.*"

The network went to a commercial and her telephone rang. She let it go to the answering machine.
She heard Mike calling her name, but she ignored
him. He hadn't told her about Trey being on his
show. It made her wonder what else he hadn't told
her.

Her telephone rang again twenty minutes later,
and again she let it go to her answering machine.

Mike's voice roared over the telephone line; aggravation tainted his words. "Holly, I know you're at home . . . answer this phone now." He paused, waiting for her to answer. "If you don't answer this phone right now, I'll come over to your house with enough noise to bring every reporter in the city on your doorstep. Now, answer this damn phone."

She was tempted, really tempted, not to answer him. But he sounded like he was serious. Holly answered the phone.

"Why the hell didn't you answer?" he yelled, when she picked up the line.

"It should be obvious. I didn't want to talk to you." Her tone was cool and distant, in total opposition to her feelings of hurt and confusion.

"I thought we agreed to calm down this afternoon," he said in an accusing manner.

"I didn't agree to anything. You just assumed that I agreed with you and left."

"Look, I don't want to fight with you," he said softly. "I called to tell you that *IE* was going to do something on us tonight."

"I saw it."

Damn. He'd hoped that she'd missed it. He wanted to tell her that he was interviewing Trey himself and not let her find out like she did. "Then you know that Trey Christian will be on my show Thursday."

She murmured a clipped, "Yes."

He sighed at her tone. "I didn't think about the interview until today. It had been set up for a while . . . before I really knew you."

"I see."

"*What* do you see?"

"I see that my life is going to be on public display again." Her voice trembled with anger and hurt. "And I don't like it."

"It's not just your life. It's my life, too."

"You *chose* to be in the spotlight. I didn't," she cried out in anger. "I was forced there by you, Trey, and even my father. I'm moving to Seattle just as soon as I can."

"What about us?" he asked in disbelief.

Pain settled in her heart like a cruel enemy. "I told you when the relationship began that I was moving. Don't pretend you didn't know."

"You'd give up our relationship and move to Seattle because of the media?"

"We have a temporary relationship, Mike."

"So our lovemaking last night meant nothing to you?" he asked with contempt. "It was just sex?"

"You know that's not the way it is," she whispered.

"Then explain to me how it is, Holly," he demanded in frustration.

"Maybe we need some time away from each other to think about this."

"There's nothing to think about. Either we have a relationship, or we don't."

Holly trembled. He was giving her an ultimatum: him, or Seattle. In her mind, she had no real choice. Seattle would always be there. Next week Mike could decide not to hang around. In her heart, Mike was the only choice. Her heart had led her astray before. Could she trust in her heart again? She was silent for a long time.

"Is it really that difficult for you, Holly?" His tone conveyed his pain. "Let me make it easy for you." He hung up the phone and her heart shattered in tiny pieces.

It was for the best, she told herself, as tears rolled down her cheeks. Now, she could get on with her life without the hassle of the media. She brushed away the tears and hung up the phone. She had gotten what she wanted, she thought to herself. So why wasn't she happy?

The next day, Holly arrived at work early. She hadn't had much sleep and the dark circles under her eyes were a testament to her sleepless night. She edged her way through the crowd of reporters at her office the same way she had when she'd left her house with a single, "No comment."

Robyn looked up from her desk when she entered. "Good morning," Holly murmured, and walked to her office. She buried herself in her work until Pam arrived.

"You look like hell. Why are you wearing that ugly black suit? What happened to the clothes with color to them?" Pam frowned in confusion and sat in the empty chair across from Holly's desk.

"Thanks, Pam. You look pretty nice yourself."

"I'm going to have to tell Mike not to keep you up so late."

Holly went still at the sound of his name. "You don't have to worry about me keeping late nights with Mike anymore."

"Oh, Holly, no." Her face filled with compassion. "What happened?"

Holly looked down at the papers on her desk,

unable to hide the pain she felt. "We just decided that we should not see each other anymore."

Pam studied her in suspicion. "Did you both decide, or did you run him off?"

"I didn't run him off," Holly replied with indignation. "I just reminded him that I was moving to Seattle regardless of our relationship."

"Real smart, Holly." Pam leaned back in the chair, folding her arms across her chest, and said sarcastically, "You finally find a man who's really attracted to you and you let your fear get in the way."

"I wasn't that attractive to him if he could drop me so quickly." Her sharp tone couldn't disguise her pain.

"Listen to yourself." Pam threw up her hands in aggravation. "I'll bet you deliberately did things just so that he would have to take a stand." Pam stood and walked to the door. "Seattle will be there, but you only have one chance at happiness with Mike. Is it worth it to you?"

Holly watched her partner walk out the door. Was it worth losing Mike? The question had nagged her all morning long. She attempted to finish the reports on her desk. Several times during the morning she'd picked up the phone to call him. What's the point, she thought. I'll still be moving. She put down the phone again.

She missed him and it was only a couple of hours since she had spoken with him.

At noon, Pam walked into her office. "Robyn and I are going out for lunch. You are coming with us. Get your purse."

"I don't really feel like going out. You go ahead."

"You can go peacefully, or we'll use force. Either way, you are coming with us."

Holly saw the determination in Pam's eyes. It wasn't worth a fight. Holly opened the desk drawer and got her purse. "Let's go."

They took two cars. Robyn drove her car to the restaurant where they planned to ditch the reporters and waited for Pam and Holly to drive up in Holly's car. They took the back exit and drove to a quiet restaurant to eat.

Pam and Robyn tried to cheer her up, but she couldn't find it in her heart to be happy today. Their food arrived and Pam excused herself. About two minutes later, Robyn followed her. Holly sat at the booth alone, waiting for the other two to return, when she saw Mike walk in the door.

Her heart raced at the sight of him. He didn't look like he had a great night's rest, either. When he reached the booth, he stopped.

"Hi," he said.

"Hi."

He nodded his head to the booth. "Can I join you?"

"Sure." She looked around the room for the others. "Pam and Robyn should be joining us soon."

"They won't be back for thirty minutes."

It sank in: she'd been set up. As much as she wanted to be angry, she couldn't be. She was glad to see him. "Oh, I see."

They were both quiet. Each studied the other with a hunger that wasn't for food.

"Holly, I love you."

Her heart stopped. She couldn't have heard him correctly. "What did you say?"

"I love you, Holly," he said softly. "I know that this is sudden and we haven't known each other long, but I know with all my heart that I love you." Mike reached across the table and took her hand. "I couldn't let things stay like they were last night."

"Mike." His name was all she could say..Surprise, joy, and pain raced through her body.

"I have something for you." He let go of her hand. Reaching inside his jacket, he removed a ring case. His hand trembled as he opened the black velvet box. The diamond solitaire sparkled in the noonday sun. "Will you marry me?"

Holly felt her heart break. With tears in her eyes, she said one word.

"No."

Holly cried as she left the restaurant. The ride back was somber. Robyn and Pam took her to Pam's house instead of the office and Pam stayed with her.

It took Holly a while to realize where she was. "I'm sorry for being such a crybaby. I'll go home now."

"You're not going home alone. You can camp out here for the day. You need someplace quiet." Pam looked at her with sympathy.

More tears streamed down her cheeks. "Thanks."

"What are friends for?"

Twelve

The next day was Thursday, the day Trey was to appear on Mike's show. She told herself she wasn't going to watch it. But that night, in bed, she joined thousands of Americans and watched his show.

She felt pain when Mike walked out on stage. Her eyes watched the screen hungrily. He didn't look as if her answer had bothered him. He seemed like the same cheerful, funny Mike Williams. When Trey came on the screen, Holly tensed. She listen as they spoke about his upcoming movie, which would premiere next Friday, and his life, now that he was married. Trey denied that his marriage was in trouble. Mike never mentioned her name. It was Trey who brought her up.

"I hear that you and Holly Aimes are dating."

The pleasant expression stayed on Mike's face. "This is my show; I ask the questions. So what's next for you, careerwise? Do you have another movie in the works?"

Trey went along with the change of subject. He tried several times to bring up Holly, but Mike deflected his questions, and in the end Trey ended up talking about his favorite subject, himself.

When the interview ended, Holly felt none of the

resentment or anger that she had felt previously when her name was in the press. Holly wondered: had she changed, or had losing Mike overshadowed all her emotions?

Holly went to work with a new determination over the next few days. She worked long hours to tire herself out before she went home. The reporters were still camped out around her house and office, but she ignored their questions and got a restraining order so that they had to stay a hundred feet away from the door of her house and fifty feet from the door of her office.

The long hours didn't help her forget Mike. At odd times during the day, she would reminisce on the hours they'd spent together, such as the day they'd spent at the park, or the times they'd watched videos at his house.

Even the announcement that they'd won the Milton Group bid didn't make her happy. It should have had her dancing in the street, but instead, she'd felt nothing when Pam had told her the news.

"You don't seem happy to hear about the bid," Pam said. "I would have thought you'd at least smile."

"I am happy."

Pam walked inside the office and closed the door behind her before marching over to Holly's desk. "You're not happy," she snapped. "You're tearing yourself up inside because you won't give yourself or Mike a chance for love."

"Pam." Holly cradled her head in her hands. "I don't want to talk about this."

"You're going to hear me tell you that you're a **fool** until *I* get tired. I'm not going to let you do this to yourself and not say anything about it." Pam sat on the edge of the desk and looked at Holly. "Hell, you can't gather enough enthusiasm for something you broke off your relationship with Mike for. What are you going to do in Seattle?"

"Work," she said firmly, as she lifted her head.

"There's more to life than work."

"It's my choice, Pam."

"It's a stupid choice and you know it. You don't even know if you'll be happy there."

"And you don't know if I'll be happy with Mike."

"At least you'd have given yourself a chance for happiness." Pam reached across the desk and touched her arm. "There are no guarantees in life, but you were happier with him than you are without him."

"My mind's made up, Pam."

"Oh, yeah?" Pam stood glaring down at Holly. "You can always change your mind."

That afternoon, she went to visit Carmen in the hospital. When she reached the room, it was empty. The nurse at the station told her that Carmen had been rushed to intensive care about an hour ago. Holly raced to the intensive care waiting room. Wanda sat alone in the room. Her eyes were red from earlier tears. Holly walked to her and sat down. She took Wanda's hand. They waited for hours. Holly called Pam later that afternoon and told her what had happened.

"Carmen had a turn for the worst this morning."

"What?"

"Yes. I'm going to stay with Wanda until the doctor comes and talks to her."

As they sat in the quiet waiting room, Holly thought about Mike. Wanda had lost her family to death, but she had lost the man she loved because of her own actions. Wanda cried silently beside her. "Holly, I don't know what I would do if she died. She's all the family I have left."

Holly wanted to tell her not to worry. Her sister would be fine, but she couldn't lie to Wanda. And she had to stop lying to herself. Moving to Seattle wouldn't make her happy. Only Mike could do that, she realized. Somehow, she would have to talk to him and win him back . . . if he would have her back.

The doctor came to talk to Wanda. Carmen's condition had stabilized and he felt that she had a good chance of recovery. Holly hugged Wanda, who cried even harder in relief. Holly vowed to never take life or love for granted.

Holly drove to her office when she left the hospital that evening. The work that lay waiting on her desk couldn't compete with her thoughts of Mike. Neither moving to Seattle, the press, nor Trey mattered as much to her as Mike's love did.

She'd been a fool to let him go, but she wasn't foolish enough not to try to win back his love. She looked at the crystal candy dish that was still full of chocolate kisses. He had won her heart despite the obstacles she had placed between him. *What if I've hurt him too deeply? What if he doesn't love me anymore?* She had to take that chance.

She could win his love by using the same persistent method he'd used to win her. If at first you don't succeed, keep asking and eventually he'll say yes. Hope filled her heart with joy. Holly grabbed her purse and went to Pam's office.

"Pam, how would you like to go shopping with me?"

Pam looked at her with disbelief. "*You* want to go shopping with me? What's the catch?"

"There is no catch. I'm going after the man that I love."

She swung her purse over her shoulder and muttered, "It's about damn time."

A few nights later, Holly dressed for the banquet for her father. She still dreaded going to these political campaign dinner-dances. But this time she was different. She dressed in a teal-green designer dress that she'd picked out herself. She didn't allow the reporters to rattle her composure. Holly realized in amazement that she didn't care. She really didn't care what they wrote about her. The people that loved and cared for her knew the truth, and that was all that was important.

Holly spotted her grandmother and walked over to her side.

"Hello, Holly. How are you, dear?" Her grandmother's eyes were filled with concern and love.

"I'm doing better."

"I heard about you and your young man. I'm sorry." Nola held out her arms and hugged Holly.

"It was my fault, Grandma." Holly stopped when a flash of light nearly blinded her. The photographer held his camera, ready to take another picture, when her sister Sandra joined them.

"Can I get a picture of the three of you together?"

Normally, Holly would have balked at the suggestion, but tonight, she knew that she could hold her own. With her arms around her grandmother and sister, Holly smiled for the camera.

Mike looked at the photograph of Holly and her family in the lifestyle section of the newspaper. She was beautiful. Mike felt a dart of pain in his heart as he remembered her refusal to marry him. Andy Kurtz sat across the table from Mike, eating a spanish omelette with enthusiasm. He'd noticed that Mike hadn't touched his. Mike had been like this all week long. Andy was glad that it was Friday. Hopefully, tonight's show would cheer Mike up.

"Who's going to be on the show tonight, Andy?"

"You know that everybody would kill me if I told. The only thing I can tell you is that all the guests are people you've interviewed before, with the exception of one, and we won't ask you to do anything too embarrassing."

Pam had helped Holly pick out the fire engine red dress that molded to her body in all the right places. She went to the hair salon late that afternoon and had her hair done the way her stylist had been bugging her for years to try. As her hair was washed and set, Holly had her nails manicured. Tonight was the most important night of her life and she didn't want to go to Mike's show without looking her best.

Holly didn't give herself a chance to think about him refusing her. All afternoon long she waited for confirmations on her special deliveries to the studio. Soon it was time for her to drive to the show.

Diane, Mike's producer, had left Holly's name at the guard station and Holly was allowed to enter. Diane met her at the door. "I hope you realize that I almost didn't let you in this place," she said. "You really hurt Mike, and all of us here hold you responsible."

Holly looked at her, "You *should* hold me responsible, but I can promise you that if he'll take me back, I'll do everything in my power to make him happy."

Diane looked at her and nodded. She led Holly through the studio and up the elevator to the executive offices of TTN. The young secretary smiled at them when they entered.

"Which room do we have?" Diane asked.

"Mr. Thomas's office," the secretary said.

"The big guy himself," Diane said in wonder, and led Holly to the office.

The room was huge. Two walls were made of glass and through them Holly could see the IBM tower and other Atlanta landmarks. Diane walked over to one of the television sets and turned it on. "We've got an hour until the show begins. Mike's already here, so I'll send someone up to get you after Denzel Washington leaves."

"Did everything arrive in time?" Holly asked anxiously.

"Yup, everything's here. Good luck." Diane walked out of the office, closing the door behind her.

Holly wandered around the room. It would be the longest sixty minutes of her life.

Mike was restless. He wanted to get this show over with. He'd decided to take a few days off and he was ready to leave. He needed to think about his future. It seemed like a cold, empty future without Holly.

He heard his cue to go out on stage. At least tonight would be the start of his vacation, he thought as he walked out on stage.

"It's Friday!" Mike said. Members of the audience clapped. "One day each year, my crew gets to run the show."

The cameraman cheered.

"If you haven't guessed yet, tonight's the night that the crew is in control." Mike laughed when he realized that Andy Kurtz was behind the camera. "Bring another camera over here," Mike said when he reached Andy. "I don't believe it! I don't believe it. Andy has on jeans. Folks, this is the man that has creases pressed into his golf shirt."

"Mike," a feminine voice filled the studio. "We're on a schedule here. Get back to work."

"Yes ma'am," Mike gave a mock salute to the control box.

Holly waited nervously backstage. The interview with Denzel Washington was almost over and she was up next. There was a break for the commercial, then Mike returned to the stage.

"My next guest is . . ." Mike looked to Diane for a cue, as he had had to do all during the show.

"It's a surprise. Have a seat and close your eyes," Diane said. One of his crew came on stage with a blindfold.

"Hey! What's this?"

"Don't worry about it Mike. Trust me."

"Trust you, huh. Okay."

When he was blindfolded, the man waved to Holly. That was her cue to go out on stage. She felt a cold block of fear in her heart.

"Hey that's your cue," a technician told her. She walked out on stage. The audience was quiet; they didn't recognize her. Holly walked across the stage and sat beside Mike.

"Okay, you can open your eyes now," the man said, and removed the blindfold. Mike opened his eyes. And for a brief second, he visibly lost his composure.

"Hello, Mike." Her voice cracked with nerves.

"Holly, what are you doing here?"

"Well, I invited myself on your show." She turned to Diane and said, "Would you send them out now."

About twenty reporters and photographers came through the rear exits. Flash units made the studio seem like it had been struck by lightning. Holly turned back to Mike, her love for him shining in her eyes.

"I wanted to say this once, so that the reporters could hear it from me." Holly kneeled on the floor beside Mike and looked into his eyes. "I love you." She removed the ring that was loose on her finger, took his hand, and slid the ring onto his finger. "Will you marry me, Mike?"

The audience went wild. A neon sign was lowered down from the ceiling. In large red letters it said, HOLLY LOVES MIKE.

Mike opened his mouth to speak but the words wouldn't come out. He pulled her into his arms and kissed her with all the need inside him. The flash units flashed and the reporters fired questions at them, but they were in a world of their own. A world of love.

Epilogue

Holly gently kissed Mike's bare chest before letting her head once again rest on top of it. She listened to the strong, steady sound of his heart. Her own heart rate had returned to normal only a few minutes ago. At midnight, they'd celebrated their one year anniversary in their own style. Holly smiled, remembering the sweet, wild loving that they'd shared.

She had barely made it back to Atlanta in time for their celebration. For the past six months, she and Pam had been traveling between Atlanta and Seattle. Wanda was now the manager of their new office in Seattle. Her sister, Carmen, had recovered fully from pneumonia. Holly, Pam, and Wanda worked hard to make their new business a success. This trip would be Holly's last for a while.

The four-carat diamond pendant that he'd given her draped around her neck and lay on his chest, creating another bond between them. Holly leisurely traced the path of the chain across Mike's warm flesh.

"Mike?"

"Uhm?"

"I didn't give you your anniversary gift." Holly arranged the warm chain around his nipple.

"I thought you gave me my gift earlier." His voice was husky with sleep.

"No." She kissed him again before she sat up. She opened a drawer in the night stand and removed a gaily wrapped box. "This is your gift."

Mike opened his eyes. He looked at the gift, then at his wife. "You didn't have to get me anything. Being married to you is like receiving a gift every day."

Holly felt as if her heart were overflowing with love for him. She swallowed back the tears that threatened to fall. She was too happy to be bothered with tears. She watched as Mike unwrapped the box and lifted the small, silver rattle. He raised his gaze to Holly. "Is this what I think it is?"

"Yes. You've got eight months of practice before our child arrives."

A few weeks later, Mike silently prayed as he sat in the waiting-room of Holly's doctor's office. Her doctor had advised Holly to have an ultrasound.

"Mr. Williams." The nurse that had taken Holly into the office motioned for Mike to follow her. "The doctor wants to see you."

"Is there anything wrong?" he asked nervously.

She smiled at him, "Nothing's wrong. Come inside."

Holly lay on an examination table. Tears flowed down her cheeks when she saw him. She smiled and held out her hand.

"Come and look, Mike," she said, her voice husky from emotion.

Mike went to her side.

"Have you ever seen an ultrasound, Mr. Williams?" Holly's doctor asked.

"No," Mike said, looking at the black and white screen.

"Let me show you your children," the doctor said with amusement.

Mike looked at the doctor, then at Holly, and said in astonishment, "Children?"

"Yes, children. See." The doctor pointed to the screen. "Here's the first, there's the second, and the third."

Mike stared at the screen. "Triplets," he said.

"Triplets," Holly answered.

"Your wife tells me that there is a history of triplets on her father's side of the family."

Holly nodded when Mike looked at her. "Grandma Nola is a triplet."

"Triplets," Mike muttered in shock.

Seven months later, Mike sat in a chair next to the hospital bed where his wife lay, safe and healthy. Yesterday, he hadn't believed that she would survive giving birth to his sons. Hell, he didn't know if *he* would survive watching her go through labor. But Holly showed more strength than he'd ever seen in anyone.

"This is it, Mike." Holly turned up the volume of the television.

"Holly Williams, wife of late-night talk show host,

Mike Williams, gave birth last night in Atlanta. The couple express-mailed *IE* the birth announcements." The leggy blonde smiled into the camera and held up the card. "It reads:

> 'MICHAEL AND HOLLY WILLIAMS
> ARE PLEASED TO ANNOUNCE
> THE BIRTH OF THEIR SONS,
> CHRISTOPHER DAVID WILLIAMS,
> DOUGLAS STEPHEN WILLIAMS,
> EDWARD ROBERT WILLIAMS.
> THEY ARRIVED AT 2:00 A.M.,
> 2:05 A.M., AND 2:10 A.M.
> RESPECTIVELY, MAY 16.
> MOTHER AND BABIES ARE FINE
> FATHER IS STILL IN SHOCK.'

FOR THE VERY BEST IN ROMANCE—
DENISE LITTLE PRESENTS!